D0707485

PLAYING
WITH
WORDS

PLAYING WITH WORDS

MARGIE GOLICK, Ph.D.

Pembroke Publishers Limited

© 1987 Pembroke Publishers Limited
528 Hood Road
Markham, Ontario

Editor — Frank English
Typesetting and design — Jay Tee Graphics Ltd.

Canadian Cataloguing in Publication Data
Golick, Margaret
  Playing with words

Includes index.
ISBN 0-921217-31-7

1. Word Games.   2. Language arts — Remedial teaching.
3. Educational games.   I. Title.

LB1576.G6 1987   371.3'97   C87-094618-8

Printed and bound in Canada
0 9 8 7 6 5 4 3 2

For Alexander Julius

Acknowledgements

Nearly everyone I know has played word games with me at some time or other, so I must acknowledge the stimulation and camaraderie of all my friends, relatives, and colleagues. My children, Jody, Jill, and Danny, all still playful, made major contributions to the games and mnemonics included here. They continue to be my favourite playmates.

I am grateful to Barbara Achenbaum for permission to print her geometry rhymes and to Arthur Rotman for inventing OIL ROM-JWOG and allowing me to to present it here.

For their contributions of games, mnemonics, or secret languages, I thank Sybil Schwartz, Barbara Bobrow, Corey Bobrow, Lissa Bobrow, Doris Caplan, Jane Churchill, Eileen Cummings, Matthew Decter, Ellyn Duschenes, Kate Garnett, Andrea Goldman, Fiona Hellstrom, Joy Hutton and Joshua Ravetch.

"The One-L Lama" by Ogden Nash from *The Looking Glass Book of Verse* edited by J.A. Smith is reprinted by permission of Curtis Brown Ltd. on behalf of the Estate of Ogden Nash; copyright © 1931, 1959 by Ogden Nash.

The activity cards are reprinted by permission of the publisher from *Junior Thinklab* by Jill Golick, Jane Churchill, and Margie Golick, Ken Weber, consultant. Copyright © 1979 by Science Research Associates (Canada) Ltd.

Contents

INTRODUCTION

One of the major preoccupations of educators these days is the development of techniques and materials to improve students' communication skills. There is a renewed concern with ways to make children and adolescents better speakers, fluent readers, and more confident writers. This concern is fueled by ominous reports in Canada and the United States of widespread illiteracy. Teachers complain of high school students who can't express themselves coherently or write a proper sentence. Newspapers report the stories of functionally illiterate high school graduates who are suing their schools for not teaching them to read. Universities are forced to offer remedial writing courses for freshmen who have no idea how to construct essays and term papers. The blame for this state of affairs has been placed on several contemporary phenomena. One of these is television. Its critics claim that children are addicted to low-quality programs at the expense of books. Working parents are also cited. When parents are unavailable and when children are in day care, there are fewer opportunities for child-adult communication — the normal impetus for language development. Lowered academic demands get some of the blame, especially where schools have to cope with large numbers of immigrants learning English as a second language, where parents may not be able to help with homework or have very different attitudes to education. Schools have been blamed, too, for reliance on computerized exams with multiple-choice questions. These eliminate the need for students to construct sentences and paragraphs to indicate their mastery of a subject. Gloomy social commentators, viewing the apparent decline in linguistic skills talk about the "erosion of the English language". Although I don't share the pessimism about the language itself, I do feel sorry for children who can't take advantage of all its resources. As a psychologist working with children who have genuine difficulty learning language-related skills, I spend much of my time thinking about effective teaching methods and materials, and advocate enriching children's language in every way possible.

The ability to use oral language skilfully is a priceless gift. Effective communication is a passport to social interaction and to intellectual endeavors of all kinds. It is an instrument for solving problems, learning new things, enhancing memory, and for organizing and classifying experiences.

Almost as important is facility with written language. For academic and vocational success, children need to learn to read for information and pleasure, to read with understanding and critical appraisal. They have to be able to use written expression with ease and precision to tell a story, express feelings, persuade, develop an argument, explain, or entertain.

Beyond the practical uses of language lie the joys, the fun of fantasy, poetry, jokes, riddles, and pure word play.

Language skill makes word play possible. Word games, in turn, further language development. They get children and adolescents talking and listening, thinking about the form and meaning of words and sentences. Furthermore, word games are fun, addictive, and a source of lifelong pleasure. Addict that I am, I use word play in my "work" with children. It has become the remedial tool I like best to get children and adolescents to develop their vocabulary, to improve their reading and spelling, and to sharpen their thinking skills.

This book is a collection of playful activities with words. No equipment other than pencil and paper is required for any of them, and many are purely oral — perfect for car trips or long waits in the doctor's office. Some of the games are games most adults played as children. I include them as reminders in case their own children, involved with television and video games, have not picked them up. In most cases, I include my own variations which I have developed in the course of 35 years of working with children. Others are games or activities I have invented or sort of invented in order to provide entertaining practice in particular skills. I offer them to busy parents and to teachers who are on the lookout for ways to enhance language skills and to have a good time in the process.

Games of Deduction

In our family we did a lot of playing. We turned everything into a game. I might say, "Guess who's coming to dinner?" and the children, when they were little, would say, "Is it Uncle Henry?" and I'd say, "No."

"Is it Auntie Rhoda?"

"No."

"Is it Johnny from next door?"

"No."

"Is it the people we met last year on vacation?"

"No."

And so on, easily exhausting the conventional "twenty questions". Over the years of family game-playing the questions got better and better and the children learned to narrow down the possibilities.

"Guess who's coming to dinner?", I'd ask; and they would say,

"Is it male?"

"No."

"Is she a relative?"

"No."

"Is it a contemporary of yours?"

"No."

"Have you ever met her?"

"No."

"Is she someone famous?"

"Yes."

"In the world of science?"

"No."

"In entertainment?"

"Yes."

In under ten questions they managed to figure out the most unlikely of events. A well-known personality from a popular TV show, who happened to be a friend of a friend of the family, was in town and was going to visit us.

To this day, when we get together with these three grown-up children who live far afield, we have maintained the tradition and still enjoy putting each other through the exercise of tracking down the surprise mystery guest.

The Twenty Questions format has become the prototype in much child-development research for evaluating children's cognitive prowess, for judging their capacity for deductive thinking, for partitioning things into categories, for reflecting on possibilities, and for mobilizing their intellectual resources.

Recently I evaluated Bobby — almost 12 — who has had a number of problems that made him an inefficient learner. He has had long-standing trouble processing verbal information and, as a result, often misunderstands directions and explanations in the classroom. But more of a handicap than this disability, was the mental passivity that resulted from it. Bobby had become accustomed to being confused, to not understanding things clearly. There was a readiness to accept fuzziness, to feel that certain things were beyond him. He showed a lack of curiosity and a reluctance to tackle anything that he thought might be hard. He seemed to think that people either knew an answer or they didn't. He had no awareness that there were certain kinds of problems whose answers they had to work at, by jogging their memory, or by combining several separate pieces of information, or by logical deduction or common sense or outright creativity. When I discussed Bobby's resistance to problem-solving with his parents, they acknowledged that they were not a game-playing family. To demonstrate that he needed experience in playing games, I engaged Bobby in a deductive game, while they watched.

"I'm thinking of a number between 1 and 10," I said. "You have to guess what it is. You can ask questions and I'll answer 'yes' or 'no'."

He began with, "Is it an odd number?"

"Yes," I said, impressed with the good question which skilfully narrowed down the possibilities.

"Is it under 5?"

"No." (long pause)
"Is it over 5?"
"Yes." (long pause)
"Is it 6?"

It was clear, then, to his parents that his powers of deduction needed considerable sharpening. One of the things I suggested, as I often do to parents, was that they spend less time helping him with his homework and more time playing with him.

TWENTY QUESTIONS

In the standard Twenty Questions game, one player thinks of something — a person, real or fictional, or an object — telling the other players if it belongs to the category of Animal, Vegetable, or Mineral. The other players try to guess the object by asking 20 or fewer questions. Answers must be "yes" or "no". No other answers are permissible (except for an occasional "maybe"). Players learn how to ask good questions that narrow the options. They learn to classify or categorize, to partition the possibilities, and, equally important, to make use of the feedback they get.

Here is the text of a game I played with a 12 year old. The reader can't ask any questions, but can try to arrive at the solution.

I announced the category: Animal.

1. Is it human? Yes.
2. Is it male? Yes.
3. Living? No.
4. Fictional? No.
5. Is it somebody famous? Yes.
6. Is he famous in science? No.
7. In the arts? Yes.
8. In painting? No.
9. In music? Yes.
10. Did he live in modern times? Yes.
11. Was he a singer? Yes.
12. Is it John Lennon? No.
13. Is it Elvis Presley? Yes.

That was pretty good to get Elvis Presley in 13 guesses. Luis used skilful questions, zeroing in on a time frame and occupation. But he used another strategy as well. He thought about what might have influenced my choice. That day was the anniversary of Elvis Presley's death and the radio had been featuring his songs all day.

Here is a game I played with an eight year old. This time I asked the questions. She said her category was Vegetable.

1. Is it growing? No.
2. Is it manufactured? Yes.
3. Is it edible? No.
4. Is it something we use? Yes.
5. Do we use it everyday? Not necessarily.
6. Do we wear it? No.
7. Is it found in the house? Yes.
8. Is it some kind of cloth? No.
9. Is it made from flowers? No.
10. Is it made from trees? Yes.
11. Is it wooden? No.
12. Is it made of paper? Yes.
13. Is it used for cleaning? No.
14. Is it for reading? Yes.
15. Is it a book? No.
16. Is it a newspaper? Yes.

"Is that it?" I asked. "No, you have to be more specific," she said.

17. Is it today's newspaper? Yes.

Twenty Questions is a high-level problem-solving game. The deductive skills can be taught to children gradually, through simpler games that are suitable for even very young children. I have gathered a set of similar word games, roughly ordered from simplest to most complex.

I SPY

Playable by children as young as two, I Spy can be used to develop vocabulary and to sharpen children's perceptual abilities. When they play the game, they learn to look carefully and to notice details around them.

To play the game, one player says "I spy with my little eye something that . . ." and adds an identifying specification. The object in question must be visible to all players. In the most elementary version of the game, players might confine themselves to colour words. For example, "I spy with my little eye something that is red." Played at the breakfast table in our kitchen, it used to sound something like this:

"Is it the breadbox?"   No.
"The napkins?"   No.
"My sweater?"   No.
"One of the apples in the bowl?"   No.
"Is it the geranium?"   No.
"Is it the strawberries in my cereal?"   Yes.

I Spy can be made increasingly complicated and can be used to develop other skills by changing the way the object is identified:

— by what it's made of;
— by shape;
— by function;
— by category;
— by beginning sound;
— by initial letter.

I Spy with my little eye something that is plastic (or wooden, or metal, or aluminum, or silver).

I Spy with my little eye something that is round (or oval, or rectangular, or shaped like a triangle).

I Spy with my little eye something that we wear (or eat, or carry things in).

I Spy with my little eye something that is a plant (or appliance, or container, or furniture).

I Spy with my little eye something that starts with the sound "sss"or "rrr", or "mmm", or "aaa").

I Spy with my little eye something that starts with the letter "b" (or "l", or "w", or "f").

I Spy with my little eye something that rhymes with "lap" (or "bear", or "nose").

I'M THINKING OF SOMETHING THAT . . .

This game differs from I Spy in that the object to be guessed does not have to be visible or even present. The game requires the players who do the guessing to make a mental search, to visualize, and to take inventory of things they know. All of the kinds of specifications used with I Spy can be used for this more cerebral guessing game.

MENTAL HIDE-AND-GO-SEEK

A poem I heard as a very young child was the inspiration for this game, played with my own children during many long car trips. The poem was about a disabled little boy and his infirm grandmother who entertained each other with long games of pretend hide-and-go-seek.

The hider can choose the locale — in the house, in the yard, on the playground, in nursery school — and the seekers have to guess where he or she is.

In the hall closet?   No.
Behind the couch?   No.
Under the dining room table?   No.
Behind the drapes?   Yes.

Both hiders and seekers learn to visualize; the hiders learn to be ingenious; the seekers learn to be systematic and specific in their questions.

COFFEE POT

This is another deductive game that calls for tracking down an activity. To "coffee pot" is to do something.

One player thinks of an activity — which can be something general, like "swimming", or something more specific, like "taking out the garbage". The other players try to guess the activity by asking questions about it. The questions must be yes or no questions; although, in my family, we always permitted, in the interest of absolute accuracy, answers like "it depends", "maybe", or "sometimes".

This sample game illustrates the kinds of questions players may ask.

"Do you coffee pot everyday?"
"Yes."
"Do you coffee pot alone?"
"Sometimes."
"Do adults coffee pot?"
"Yes."
"Do adults coffee pot with children?"
"Sometimes."
"Do you coffee pot at school?"
"No."
"Do you coffee pot at home?"
"Yes."
"Do you coffee pot in the daytime?"
"Yes."
"Do you coffee pot at night?"
"No."
"Do you like to coffee pot?"
"Yes."
"Is coffee potting good for you?"
"Yes."
"Do you need special equipment to coffee pot?"
"Sort of."
"Do you coffee pot outdoors?"
"No."
"Do you coffee pot in the basement?"
"No."
"Do you coffee pot in your bedroom?"
"No."
"Do you coffee pot in the kitchen?"
"Yes."
"Is it cooking?"
"No."
"Is it eating?"
"Be more specific."
"Is it eating breakfast?"
"Yes."

RIDDLES

"Riddles" is the cover term I am using for conventional riddles, conundrums, brain teasers, and all kinds of word games that call for a verbal solution to a problem posed by an interlocutor.

A part of the culture of childhood, riddles are the stuff of intellectual activity. Here are some riddles children have asked me lately.

Q. How can you make a slow horse fast?
A. Stop feeding him.

Q. Why did the farmer call his pig ink?
A. Because it kept running out of the pen.

Q. What's the difference between a teacher and a railway conductor?
A. A teacher trains the mind and a conductor minds the train.

Q. Why is a riddle like a pencil?
A. It's no good without a point.

Frivolities? No. The fact that riddles and riddling have been handed down for centuries suggests that they must have a useful function in mental development. There are many kinds of benefits that come to the riddler. The question-and-answer format teaches turn-taking — the most important rule of conversation. It is a kind of rehearsal for innumerable situations in life where the child is asked to respond to a question, or even where that child has to have the courage or the self-confidence to ask a question. The specific benefits to language development come from the content. Riddles demand and therefore develop particular kinds of linguistic awareness.

Some riddles depend on phonological awareness — a sensitivity to the sounds of words. These are riddles where the humour is based on similarities of sound. They encourage children to think about the phonological structure of words; that is, the sounds of which they are composed.

Q. What happens when ducks fly upside down?
A. They quack up.

Q. Why is a pig's tail like getting up at four o'clock in the morning?
A. Because it's twirly.

Q. How do you keep from starving in the desert?
A. Eat the sandwiches there.

Another kind of riddle is based on puns. To understand them, children have to develop an awareness of the ambiguity in words, to learn about homonyms, and to expand their stock of words with multiple meanings. Some examples of this kind of riddle are:

Q. Why is it always cool in a baseball stadium?
A. Because there's a fan in every seat.

Q. Why does a sick person lose the sense of touch?
A. Because he doesn't feel well.

Q. Why couldn't the animals play cards on the Ark?
A. Because Noah sat on the deck.

Then there are the riddles based on grammatical ambiguity — alternative interpretations of the same sentence structure.

Q. What kind of animal can jump higher than a house?
A. Any animal. Houses can't jump.

Metalinguistic riddles are particularly tricky. They call for shifting attention from the content, that is, the meaning of the words, to their structure, the elements of which they are composed. For example,

Q. What occurs once in a minute, twice in a moment, and not once in a hundred years?
A. The letter M.

Q. What starts with E, ends with E, and has one letter in it?
A. An envelope.

Q. What do Winnie-the-Pooh and John the Baptist have in common?
A. Their middle name.

All of these kinds of riddles make children think about how language works and practise and refine their verbal skills. Equally important are the problem-solving skills that riddles foster: looking inside oneself, stirring up of thought processes, and re-arranging ideas to try to come up with an answer — particularly important for youngsters who, accustomed to "not knowing", tend to sink into passivity.

Especially good for promoting problem-solving, are those riddles that are not based on word play, but pose a genuine intellectual challenge. These riddles call for divergent thinking — getting out of a rut and seeing things in new ways.

Q. How can you carry water in a sieve?
A. Freeze it.

Q. Why is it easier to clean a mirror than a window?
A. You only have to clean one side.

Q. What is smaller than an atom, larger than the Universe, eaten by dead people, but if you eat it, you die?
A. Nothing.

All of the varieties of riddles help to cultivate a number of faculties that are essential to success at school. These include:

(1) *Careful listening*. This calls for paying attention to all of the information in a message, listening to the very end, not jumping the gun, discriminating among similar sounds, noticing little words that have important semantic consequences, and registering and remembering the sequence of words where order determines meaning.

(2)*Thinking through a solution*. Too many children have a kind of passivity when confronted with a question where the answer is not immediately obvious. When asked, in the course of an intelligence test, some question of common-sense judgement, like "What should you do if you lose a ball that belongs to one of your friends?", they are apt to say, "I don't know." No amount of prompting can convince them that they can figure out an answer through reason or imagination. Questions of opinion, logic, or judgement are treated in the same way as questions of fact. "I don't know," might be a sensible answer to "Who discovered America?" Even with that kind of question, there are some children and adolescents who, although they don't have the answer on the tip of their tongue, are willing to make the effort to track it down in their own memory bank. "Let's see, it wasn't Jacques Cartier. It was this Spanish or Italian guy. Wait a second, wait a second . . . Columbo!"

(3) *A willingness to combine several kinds of information to form hypotheses, to test them, reject them where necessary, and to persist in their efforts at a solution.*

And, most important of all, when children learn riddles, understand them, ask or answer them, they are being initiated into an important childhood ritual. As initiates, they can go on to share in a rich mine of *memorable* information.

I underline "memorable" because children forget so much of the information fed to them in classroom situations or can't retrieve it when they need it. I was once assessing a seven year old who was doing poorly in school and was said to have problems with memory. In the course of giving her a standardized achievement test, I had asked her the question "Who invented the airplane?" She said, with no hesitation, "The Wright brothers." Surprised, I asked, "How did you know that?"

"From the riddle," she said.

"What riddle?" I asked.

"Who invented the first airplane that couldn't fly?"

"What's the answer?"

"The Wrong brothers."

RHYMING GAMES

Reading theoreticians and researchers have long suspected a link between children's sensitivity to rhyme and the phonological skills essential in becoming a good reader. It is in taking words apart and noting the separate phonetic segments of which a word is composed that children discover how writing maps onto speech. Recently two British researchers, Bradley and Bryant*, demonstrated the important role these abilities play in learning to read. Moreover, they showed that the development of these skills, when lagging, can be speeded up.

Parents can enhance this skill in pre-schoolers by reading nursery rhymes and by playing rhyming and alphabet games. I have used games like these in my work with children with learning disabilities to help them develop the metalinguistic skills of rhyming, alliteration, and alphabetizing. Most of the games I know come from my childhood, from play with my own children and their friends. Their value as a remedial tool comes from their status as games rather than academic exercises. Children who learn them from an adult go on to play them with other children. Once the game is in their repertoire they think about it, play it in their heads, and store up strategies to dazzle their friends in the next round of play.

---

*L. Bradley and P. Bryant. *Rhyme and Reason in Reading and Spelling.* Ann Arbor: University of Michigan Press, 1985.

In all of the games, the problem-solving element is paramount.
While learning to rhyme, to isolate beginning and ending sounds, and to alphabetize, the players are learning to solve problems. And while solving them, they are thinking about words, learning the meanings of new ones, learning new facts, stretching their memories, and strengthening their powers of concentration.

STINKY PINKY

This game has acquired more elegant names since I first played it as a child, but this is the name I knew and the name by which I have introduced it to hundreds of children and teachers whose mothers didn't play it with them.

The game requires two or more players. One player thinks up a rhyming pair of words and provides a verbal clue — a non-rhyming definition. The other player(s) must discover the rhyming word pair. The example that comes immediately to mind from my childhood games is this one.

Player A: Obese feline animal

Player B: fat cat

I actually remember, at the age of seven or eight, learning the meaning of the words "obese" and "feline" in this context.

The game encourages careful listening to the clue and narrowing down the possibilities for an answer, constrained by the syntax of the clue and the need to find rhyming words. I have tailored the game to the needs of beginning readers, adding a dimension that develops phonics skills, encourages reading, and allows for hints or prompts so that the child nearly always arrives at the solution. What I have done is create a list of "easy reading" rhymes and rhymes that highlight spelling patterns that I want my students to learn. I give the clue verbally or in writing — depending on the occasion, or the needs or abilities of the players. If they can't come up with the response on the basis of the verbal clue alone, I provide spaces for the letters in each word, then write in key letters. It might be the initial letters, or the final letters, or the median vowel.

My collection follows, with occasional sample hints. Some definitions are particularly suitable for upper elementary school children and adolescents who have a wider vocabulary than those in the earliest years of school.

CONSONANT-VOWEL-CONSONANT WORD PAIRS

1. He's been sitting in the sun.
2. My puppy fell in the tub.
3. The truck that delivers Campbell's soup. (c— ——)
4. I was there when the plane got in. (m— j—)
5. Everyone is playing with water pistols. (–u– –u–)
6. What you say to the racers after "Ready"
7. Nancy knows how to do it.
8. Introduced to the animal doctor (m— v—)
   -or an alternative definition for older students
   — Experienced opera singer (M— v—)
9. Chief of Police
10. Large toupee
11. What we won at the dog show (–up ——)
12. Dogcatcher's tool (–et –et)
13. A run in the swamp (b— j—)
14. Baby's crib (t— c—)
15. Naughty boy (b— ——)
16. Where the chickens are kept (—— –en)
17. Sizzling pan
18. Sliced almond
19. I broke my tooth on the olive. (b— p—)
20. Two male basketball teams (–e– ––n)
21. I can't blow bubbles with this.(b— g—)
22. Gloomy parents (two rhyming pairs required)
    (––d ——; gl— ——)

COMPLEX VOWEL SPELLINGS

23. Recipe source
24. Groovy chair
25. Satisfactory lumber
26. We all eat out of the same bowl.
27. Loyal, brave, true, prepared, and fat (––ou– ––ou–)
28. Heat up the grease. (–oi– oi–)
29. Lamp for the dark (–igh– –igh–)
30. The men in armour had a battle.
31. The funny man at the circus fell off the ladder.
    (––ow– –ow–)
32. It's almost lunch time. (–oo– –oo–)

33. Where I keep my cleaning tools (br--m ----)
34. The spot I got on my dress when I wore it in the wet. (-ain -----)
35. What Little Bo Peep can't seem to do
36. Mark on the grass left there by an animal with his house on his back
37. What you do when you have roast beef for dinner (--- ----)
38. Boss of the robbers (ch---- --ie-)

SILENT E THAT MAKES VOWELS LONG

39. Artificial pond
40. Chief aircraft (-ai- --a-e)
41. What you do when company is coming (-a-e -a-e)
42. Pleasant rodents (--ce ----)
43. What two ladies called Mary have in common (s--- n---)
44. Just a snack (-igh- -i-e)
45. Female horses like this are scarce. (r--- m---)

DIGRAPHS, CONSONANT CLUSTERS

46. Seafood plate (--sh ----)
47. Ailing hen (--ck ---ck)
48. Fruit drink to go with sandwiches (l---ch p----)
49. Why my brother won the weightlifting contest (--st ---st)
50. Noisy group (-ou- cr---)
51. The animal who keeps stealing the robins' eggs (--st p---)
52. One more charge and we're all through dynamiting.(l--- b----)
53. Strawberry-flavoured lemonade (--nk ---nk)
54. We can't get our van out of the mud. (st--- ----ck)
55. Fee for the campsite (t--- r---)
56. Tune that goes on forever (--ng ----)
57. What the queen says when she wants her husband to serenade her
58. The girl that I married was too fat to get through the door.
59. Get me what I need for my kite. (br--- -------)
60. Geologist's lecture (----- -alk)
61. Extra seat (sp--- --ai-)
62. Ancient valuable shiny metal
63. Hyperactive youngster (----- ch---)

R-COLOURED VOWELS

64. The wheels are burning.
65. Medicine that's certain to work
66. The light in the sky is a billion kilometres away.
67. The playground at night (----- p----)
68. Tennis or racquet ball (c--r- --ort)
69. Noted the sound of the chickadee (-ear- -ir-)
70. Spots on my blouse (--ir- d----)

FINAL CONSONANTS THAT DOUBLE

71. What my mother wants to see in my room (--ss --ss)
72. Who is going to fetch a pail of water with Jack? (--ll --ll)
73. Tiny bouncer (--all ----)
74. What the dictionary helps you do (sp--- --ll)
75. Angry employer (cr--- ----)
76. Tension caused by checkmating (ch--- str---)

-ER ENDINGS

77. The one who puts the crackers in the box (------er p-------)
78. Better knife (n--er -------)
79. Dehydrated fish soup (ch----er p------)
80. Boxer who lost weight (l------- -----er)
81. What I said in the restaurant when asked if I wanted my coffee with the meal (l--er w------)
82. More ancient rock (----er -oul---)
83. What I'd like for my shower (h----er w----)
84. Advocate of male poultry (---ster b-------)
85. Improved pullover (b------ s-------)

PLURALS, POSSESSIVES, APOSTROPHES

86. Robert's chores
87. Doctor's helper's handbags (------'s p-----s)
88. Samuel's berets (----'s ----s)
89. Stanley's proposals (----'- ------)
90. Poet's deck (b----'s -ar---)

MISCELLANEOUS

91. Extraordinary worms (gr---- b----)
92. Peculiar coins (f----- m-----)
93. Chewing gum that won't stay still (w----ly Wr-------)
94. Suspicious-looking parson (s-------- m--------)
95. Not the first violin, nor the third violin, but the one in between. (--dd-- -------)
96. Lollypop dropped on the beach
97. Couturiers to the navy (s----ors' t----ors)
98. Stretchy synthetic material (e------- pl------c)
99. A better kite (h----er f---er)
100. Adam's wife's clothing (E---'s -------)

STINKY PINKY ANSWERS

1. tan man (other guesses have included "red Fred" and "yellow fellow"
2. wet pet (soggy doggy)
3. can van
4. met jet
5. gun fun
6. get set
7. Nan can
8. met vet or Met vet
9. top cop (head Fed; big pig)
10. big wig
11. pup cup
12. pet net
13. bog jog
14. tot cot
15. bad lad
16. hen pen
17. hot pot
18. cut nut
19. bit pit
20. ten men
21. bum gum
22. sad dad; glum mum

23. cook book
24. neat seat (cool stool)
25. good wood (fine pine)
26. group soup (clan pan)
27. stout scout (chubby hubby)
28. boil oil
29. night light
30. knight fight
31. clown down
32. soon noon
33. broom room
34. rain stain
35. keep sheep
36. snail trail
37. eat meat
38. chief thief
39. fake lake
40. main plane
41. bake cake
42. nice mice
43. same name
44. light bite
45. rare mare
46. fish dish
47. sick chick (In Australia, "crook chook")
48. lunch punch
49. best chest
50. loud crowd
51. nest pest
52. last blast
53. pink drink
54. stuck truck
55. tent rent
56. long song
57. sing, King
58. wide bride
59. bring string
60. rock talk
61. spare chair
62. old gold

63. wild child
64. tire fire
65. sure cure
66. far star
67. dark park
68. court sport
69. heard bird
70. shirt dirt
71. less mess
72. Jill will
73. small ball
74. spell well
75. cross boss
76. chess stress
77. cracker packer
78. nicer slicer
79. chowder powder
80. lighter fighter
81. later, Waiter
82. older boulder
83. hotter water
84. rooster booster
85. better sweater
86. Bob's jobs
87. nurse's purses
88. Sam's tams
89. Stan's plans
90. bard's cards
91. great bait
92. funny money
93. wiggly Wrigley
94. sinister minister
95. middle fiddle
96. sandy candy
97. sailors' tailors
98. elastic plastic
99. higher flyer
100. Eve's leaves

GEOGRAPHY RHYMES

Rhymes like these are meant to be used with a map. Those who know the place names well and are good at rhyming won't need the map — although finding the city, once they have discovered its name, may improve their map skills. For many children, however, completion of the rhyme will be a problem-solving task and one which engages them actively in studying the map, in learning the names of towns and cities in a country, and in learning how to spell them.

My rhymes were created for children who were studying Canadian geography. I used them with children who generally had a hard time learning new labels for things — or, at least, had trouble retrieving a name on demand. When asked for the capital city of Canada or the largest city in British Columbia, they knew they "knew" it, but couldn't produce it on the spot. Having to figure out a name with the rhyming clues, makes it more memorable. The entire rhyme then acts as a prompt to help retrieve that name when necessary. For some of the children, having a game to play was the incentive that made the geography lesson tolerable.

These rhymes are simply guidelines for children, teachers, and parents who, I hope, will make their own rhymes to suit their own learning and teaching needs.

Whenever I want to catch a fish,
I see my aunt in A ---------- (town in Nova Scotia)

Wear a scarf around your neck
When it's windy in Q------ (capital city of one of the Canadian provinces)

Unless it's summer, spring or fall,
Don't spend a month in M--------.(city in Quebec)

Things get done
In E--------.(city in Alberta)

M-------- Hat, M-------- Hat, (town in Alberta)
How did it get a name like that?

Remember, if your journey
Is not the way you planned,
S----- J---- is in New Brunswick,
S----- J----'s in Newfoundland.

There's a place to snuggle up with a favourite story book;
It's a cosy little corner in a town called C————— —————.
(city in Newfoundland)

Every Newfoundlander
Goes to visit G——————. (town in Newfoundland)

If things are dull,
Then go to H————. (city in Quebec)

It oughta be against the law
To raise your voice in O——————. (Capital city)

If you have a wooden leg,
Watch your step in W—————————.(city in Manitoba).

Charlotte wore a golden gown,
Charlotte went to C———————————. (city in Prince Edward Island)
After that she took a ride
And found herself in S——————————. (city in Prince Edward Island)

I found a wife
In Y———————————. (city in the Northwest Territories)

Call me if you need a mover;
My van is parked in West V——————————. (city in British Columbia).

In New York
They use a fork;
They use a spoon
In S——————————. (city in Saskatchewan)

Dark horse or light horse,
Take me straight to W———————————. (city in Yukon)

Whether Liberal or Tory, ya
Can't beat V—————————. (city in British Columbia)

The world's finest speller
Plays the drum in D———————————. (city in Alberta)

A big bee
In D————— (town in Nova Scotia)
Stung me on the nose.
The big bee
In D————— (as above)
Thought it was a rose.

I call my sweetheart "ma cherie"
When I go to C-----------. (town in Quebec)

I'd go through thick and thin to stay
A week or two in T------- B--. (city in Ontario).

Try to get your teacher to take you to T-------, (city in Ontario)
That's the place that you can do anything you want to.

Pete is thrifty,
Pete is thorough,
He's my pal
In P------------. (city in Ontario).

You oughta go to O------;
That's the place to see
The Royal Mint and Parliament
And the National Gallery. (city in Ontario)

I met a man in H-------, (city in Nova Scotia)
He showed me how he played his sax.
He played it hot, he played it cool,
And then he went to L---------. (town in Nova Scotia)

GEOGRAPHY RHYME ANSWERS

Antigonish
Quebec
Montreal
Edmonton
Medicine Hat
Saint John, Saint John's
Corner Brook
Gander
Hull
Ottawa
Winnipeg
Charlottetown, Summerside
Yellowknife

Vancouver
Saskatoon
Whitehorse
Victoria
Drumheller
Digby
Chicoutimi
Thunder Bay
Toronto
Peterborough
Ottawa
Halifax, Liverpool

COMMITTEE LIMERICKS

They say a camel is a horse designed by a committee. Maybe a committee is not the most efficient way to create something, but in this game everyone has fun pooling their talents to create limericks.

Each player gets pencil and paper. Each writes the first line of a limerick. Papers are passed to the left after each line is written. Each player adds a suitable second line to the first line on the paper, and so on, until a traditional five-line limerick has been completed. The final versions are read aloud in turn.

The more players, the merrier the game. It is best played in "mixed" company, that is, with adults and children, so that the more able poets can help the less able with rhyme scheme, rhythm, and the occasional rhyming word. There is always at least one player in every crowd — frequently an adult — who cannot quite get the hang of the limerick formula. In our family we permit players to change each other's lines slightly in the interest of improving the final product. Permissible changes include adding or deleting a syllable or two, changing the sentence structure slightly, and, in rare cases, even changing the final word for a more easily rhymable synonym.

If some of the players have no experience with limericks, it will be important to read some aloud, teach the rhyme scheme and rhythm, and give practice in producing first and third lines. In traditional limericks, the first, second, and fifth lines rhyme; and the third and fourth lines rhyme. The first, second, and fifth lines have three beats each and the third and fourth each have two beats.

See the Spelling and Math rhymes (pp. 89 and 94) for some sample limericks — not written by a committee. Here, on the other hand, are some limericks produced in some lively committees.

There once was a white furry rabbit
Who had a ridiculous habbit;
When he wanted a carrot
And no one would share it,
He'd reach with a fork and he'd stab it.

I wish that you'd leave me alone
And not call me up on the phone.
I'm terribly busy,
These calls make me dizzy,
So do me a favour, call Joan.

Macaroni for dinner — how nice,
Though we've had it this week at least twice.
When I see all that pasta
My heart beats much faster;
It's a hundred times better than rice.

When Goldilocks saw the three bears
She ran fast as she could down the stairs.
"Thank goodness I'm free,"
She shouted with glee,
"But I'm sorry I broke all their chairs."

Sometimes, particularly if there are many novices at the game, it helps to supply a variety of first lines. These can be used, too, for a variation on the game. In this version, all players begin with the same first line, and each produces a limerick. The variety of themes that the same first line produces is often very surprising. Players — even old friends — amaze each other with their originality and ingenuity.

Here are ten first lines that lend themselves to lots of good rhyming possibilities:

In an evil old castle in Spain

I like butter and jam on my toast

A lady who loved to ride horses

Thirty-three thirsty raccoons

On a cold snowy Sunday last spring

Said a hungry young boy to his mum

There was a tycoon from New York

There's a house at the top of a hill

An astronaut went to the moon

I really don't think it is fair

ALPHABET GAMES

I am always on the lookout for game-like activities that get children to notice the arrangement of letters within words, that get them to take words apart and put them together again, and that force them to think about spelling, about sounds and about relationships among words.

The simplest such activity is the "Wonder Word" game (also called "Word Search") often found in newspapers, comic books, and children's activity books. There is a square of letters that contain words arranged horizontally, vertically, and diagonally. The players are required to find all the hidden words, marking them off from all the distracting letters that surround them. In the easiest versions, the words to be found are listed on the side, and players — even those who cannot spell the words — must simply seek out the specified arrangement of letters. Playing the game draws attention to the order of letters in words.

More demanding games of this kind call for finding a particular set of words without a list of the words to be found — say kinds of animals, or Canadian provinces and territories, or all of the United States. The words are all there, but players have to do some looking inside themselves to prompt or verify their searches.

The most demanding of this kind of game is the genuine Crossword Puzzle, where each word filled in is constrained by semantic clue, number of letters, and the letters that will satisfy the clues that intersect. Crossword puzzles give a real workout to language facility, spelling abilities, and problem-solving skills. Crossword puzzles are made at every conceivable level of difficulty, from those suitable for the beginning reader to those that will challenge the most erudite and experienced lover of word games.

There are commercial games that offer some of the challenges of the paper-and-pencil game. These are games with letter tiles: Scrabble and Junior Scrabble, Perquackey, and Boggle. All involve the players in arranging and rearranging letters to make words. Players can't help expanding their vocabularies and improving their spelling.

The games I will discuss are non-commercial games — some purely oral, some requiring paper and pencil — all of which have been handed down for generations, all of which are fun, all of which involve players with sound, with sense, with spelling, and with problem solving.

GEOGRAPHY

When I was growing up this was the game we played on car trips. I spent hours consulting atlases in secret to augment my store of geography "names" — cities, counties, countries, continents, lakes, rivers, oceans. In travels with my own children, Geography was a standby. Just as today's pre-schoolers learn to isolate beginning and ending sounds from "Sesame Street", my children, 20 years ago, learned that skill from endless games of Geography. In this game, the first player gives a geographical name — a city, county, country, continent, lake, river, ocean, mountain, etc. The next player must give one that begins with the last letter of the first player's word and so on. The object of the game is to stump the other players. No names may be repeated in the course of a game. The player who cannot produce a name beginning with the required letter is out of the game and his or her turn passes to the next player. Here is a sample — a number of rounds from a recent game I played with three children, ranging in age from six to fourteen.

Player A: Canada
Player B: Afghanistan
Player C: New York
Player D: Kentucky
        A: Yarmouth
        B: Halifax
        C: Xanadu
        D: Xanadu's not a real place.
        C: Yes it is. It's in Africa.
        D: Uruguay
        A: Yugoslavia
        B: Argentina
        C: Alberta
        D: Alps
        A: South America
        B. Australia
        C. Austria
        D. Amazon

ONE AT A TIME

Lewis Carroll may have invented this word game. The player is challenged to turn a specified word into another specified word in a specified number of moves by changing only one letter at a time. Each letter change must produce a real word. A number of challenges of this kind are included in *Lewis Carroll's Bedside Book**. Caleb Gattegno****, innovative educator and creator of *Words in Color*, an ingenious and comprehensive method of teaching reading, includes "Games of Transformation" like these to draw children's attention to the structure of words. Over the years, in this kind of play with children, I have accumulated my own stock of word pairs that can be turned into each other. The words are familiar, easy to read, and easy to spell. This is generally true, too, of the words that are formed in the process of change.

---

* E. Cuthwellis (Ed.). *Lewis Carroll's Bedside Book*. Boston: Houghton-Mifflin, 1979.
** C. Gattegno. *Words in Color*. New York: Educational Solutions, 1977.

Many of the pairs can be introduced to children who are still at the very early stages of skill with written language, reading and spelling only words of the form consonant-vowel-consonant. Others help to reinforce the ability to read and spell consonant blends, digraphs, and exceptional spellings.

Here are my favourite challenges. In each case the solution given is only one of several possibilities. Undoubtedly some players will provide better solutions to some of the challenges and produce the changes in even fewer moves than I did.

1. HAT to CAP in 2 moves
2. BOY to MAN in 3 moves
3. HIM to HER in 2 moves
4. HUG to HIT in 2 moves
5. SUN to HOT in 4 moves
6. BOX to BAG in 3 moves
7. SIX to TEN in 3 moves
8. MILK to WINE in 3 moves
9. LOVE to HATE in 3 moves
10. PITCH to CATCH in 2 moves
11. MAT to RUG in 3 moves
12. CAT to DOG in 3 moves
13. MOM to DAD in 4 moves
14. MOTHER to FATHER in 3 moves
15. COLD to WARM in 4 moves
16. SHIP to BOAT in 5 moves
17. HARD to SOFT in 5 moves
18. BOY to LAD in 3 moves
19. BOY to GAL in 3 moves
20. CUP to MUG in 6 moves
21. SICK to WELL in 4 moves
22. EAST to WEST in 3 moves
23. HIDE to FIND in 4 moves
24. WET to DRY in 5 moves
25. RIDE to WALK in 6 moves
26. EYE to EAR in 8 moves
27. FLY to BEE in 5 moves
28. CAR to BUS in 4 moves
29. LAMB to MARY in 7 moves
30. PEAR to PLUM in 6 moves

31. FAST to SLOW in 9 moves
32. DEAD to LIVE in 7 moves
33. BRAT to DEAR in 4 moves
34. VAST to TINY in 7 moves
35. RICH to POOR in 9 moves
36. NONE to SOME in 3 moves
37. OLD to NEW in 9 moves
38. NOSE to TOES in 4 moves
39. HEAT to COLD in 4 moves
40. PLAY to WORK in 8 moves
41. COIN to BILL in 5 moves
42. JACK to KING in 5 moves
43. SPADE to HEART in 5 moves
44. TWO to SIX in 5 moves

ONE AT A TIME ANSWERS

1. HAT CAT CAP
2. BOY BAY MAY MAN
3. HIM HEM HER
4. HUG HUT HIT
5. SUN NUN NUT HUT HOT
6. BOX BOY BAY BAG
7. SIX SIN TIN TEN
8. MILK MINK WINK WINE
9. LOVE LAVE LATE HATE
10. PITCH PATCH CATCH
11. MAT RAT RAG RUG
12. CAT COT COG DOG
13. MOM MOP MAP MAD DAD
14. MOTHER BOTHER BATHER FATHER
15. COLD CORD CARD WARD WARM
16. SHIP CHIP CHAP CHAT COAT BOAT
17. HARD HART PART PORT SORT SOFT
18. BOY BAY LAY LAD
19. BOY BAY GAY GAL
20. CUP CUT CAT HAT HAG HUG MUG
21. SICK SILK SILL SELL WELL
22. EAST LAST LEST WEST
23. HIDE HIRE FIRE FINE FIND
24. WET PET PAT PAY PRY DRY

25. RIDE TIDE TIME TAME TALE TALK WALK
26. EYE RYE ROE HOE HOT HAT MAT EAT EAR
27. FLY SLY SHY SHE SEE BEE
28. CAR BAR BAT BUT BUS
29. LAMB LAME CAME COME CORE MORE MARE MARY
30. PEAR PEAL SEAL SEAM SLAM SLUM PLUM
31. FAST PAST PART PORT FORT FOOT BOOT BLOT BLOW SLOW
32. DEAD LEAD LEND FEND FIND FINE FIVE LIVE
33. BRAT BRAN BEAN BEAR DEAR
34. VAST VASE VANE MANE MINE MINT TINT TINY
35. RICH RICE RACE PACE PACT PART PORT POUT POUR POOR
36. NONE CONE COME SOME
37. OLD ODD ADD AND AID BID BED FED FEW NEW
38. NOSE LOSE LOSS TOSS TOES
39. HEAT HEAD HELD HOLD COLD
40. PLAY SLAY SLAT SEAT PEAT PEAK PERK PORK WORK
41. COIN COIL BOIL BAIL BALL BILL
42. JACK PACK PICK PINK PING KING
43. SPADE SPARE SPARS SEARS HEARS HEART
44. TWO TOO TON SON SIN SIX

WORDS WITHIN WORDS

Find the little words in the big words. Don't change the order or the position of any letters. Only words of two or more letters are permitted.

This is an activity often found in spellers and workbooks, drawing children's attention to the order of letters in words and to the presence of "silent" or ambiguous letters. The active involvement of looking closely at a familiar word and hunting for patterns within it, leads to better spelling skills. If interesting words are chosen, this activity can be presented as a game with a time limit or a challenge.

In my work with children with learning disabilities it has proved a boon to those children who are slow to discover spelling patterns in words. After playing the game, they remember tricky spelling like the "or" in "work"; the "on" in the "-tion" suffix or the "the" in "thermometer". It helps, too, to make more concrete and familiar the "function" words that have no real meaning in isolation, but important grammatical significance — words like "the", "is", "on", "of", "at", etc.

1. potato (find four words)
2. carrot (find two words)
3. stringbean (find six words)
4. chocolate (four words)
5. pineapple (four words)
6. omelet (two words)
7. scrambled (nine words)
8. watermelon (seven words)
9. mother (four words)
10. grandfather (seven words)
11. restaurant (four words)
12. outdoor (five words)
13. stubborn (four words)
14. pillow (three words)
15. tear (two words)
16. peanut butter (five words—not counting "peanut" and "butter")
17. thermometer (seven words)
18. television (four words)
19. airplane (five words)
20. often (two words)
21. teacher (five words)
22. coffee (three words)
23. some (two words)
24. important (six words)
25. information (nine words)

WORDS WITHIN WORDS ANSWERS

1. pot tat at to
2. car rot
3. string ring in bean be an
4. cola late ate at
5. pine pin in apple
6. me let

47

7. cram ram am amble ambled bled led ramble rambled
8. water at ate term melon me on
9. moth her he the
10. grand father and fat at the her
11. rest ran rant aura
12. out door do outdo or
13. stub born tub or
14. pill ill low
15. tea ear
16. pea nut but an utter
17. the her mom meter mete met me
18. vision is on ion
19. air plane plan an lane
20. of ten
21. teach each tea ache her
22. off of fee
23. so me
24. import imp port or ant tan
25. inform in form for or format mat ion on

MY GRANDMOTHER LIKES APPLES BUT SHE DOESN'T LIKE PEARS

In this game, also known as Chilli Williams Is a Very Strange Girl, one player, already initiated into the rules, challenges a number of uninitiated players to figure out Grandmother's other likes and dislikes. The challenger simply announces items, always pairing a pro and a con, e.g.,

My grandmother likes coffee, but she doesn't like tea.
She likes beer, but she doesn't like wine.
She likes butter, but not margarine.
. . . cherries, but not grapes.
. . . skiing, but not skating.
. . . letters, but not postcards.
. . . rolls, but not bread.
. . . running, but not walking.

When one of the players has a hypothesis, he or she asks a question: "Does she like raisins?"

The challenger may answer, "No, but she likes currants."

As soon as a player correctly designates Grandmother's likes (has five consecutive questions that are answered with "yes"), that player joins the challenger in answering the questions, giving the examples. Play continues until all players have discovered the source of Grandmother's pleasure.

The game is played orally, but a player who is unable to arrive at a solution should be encouraged to keep a written record of Grandmother's likes and dislikes. It might look like this,

Likes	Dislikes
food	drink
Russia	Roumania
sitting	standing
seeing	hearing
books	magazines
ballet	tap
jazz	rock
tennis	golf
baseball	hockey
dessert	soup
Apple	Atari
Queens	Kings

Eventually it becomes apparent that Grandmother likes anything with a double letter in it.

Other versions have been created by ingenious players. For example,

Grandmother only likes things without the letter E in them (she'll ride a pony, but not a horse; she'll keep a cow, but not cattle, etc.).

Grandmother only likes things spelled with three letters (She'll drive a car, but not an automobile; she'll eat ham, but not beef; she'd rather be fat than thin, etc.).

SIGN GAME

In our family, we always played an alphabet game in the car. In this game, each player has to spot and call out a word anywhere in the environment, visible on signs, billboards, or licence plates, that begins with each of the letters of the alphabet in turn. The first player to go through the alphabet is the winner. In some versions of the game, players are allowed to use letters that are actually part of a car's licence number.

The game encourages visual alertness and fast reactions. Only the first player to spot a key letter is allowed to use it. Thus, if two players are looking for C at the same time, only the first one to call out "Coke", having seen the billboard coming into view, can count the C.

All of my children developed an excellent memory for the environment. Anyone who had gotten as far as W was always ready for the Xerox plant when it came into view. On trips to places that we visited often, we varied the game, starting with Z and working back to A.

I LOVE MY LOVE WITH AN A

Here are several versions of a game that is useful in stimulating vocabulary development in children and adolescents, in encouraging them to expand their knowledge of the world, stretch their memories, and practise phonic skills and alphabetizing. The first player says "I love my love with an A because he (or she) is . . ." Then, depending on the version played, she adds an adjective, or an occupation, or a nationality beginning with the letter. The next player repeats the formula with the letter B, and so on. There is a version that incorporates a memory element. Each player recapitulates everything said by the previous players before adding his or her letter. This encourages careful listening and helps players discover the effectiveness of initial-letter prompts in expanding their capacity to remember lists.

Here are some sample games. (These games present good opportunities to break down, by discussion and example, the stereotypes of sexism and racism.)

50

OCCUPATIONS

I love my love with an A because he's/she's an accountant.
I love my love with a B because he's/she's a baseball player.
(The formula is always repeated when the game is played, but to save space only the occupations are given here.)

. . . a carpenter
. . . a doctor
. . . an engineer
. . . a farmer
. . . a gardener
. . . a housekeeper
. . . an inside agent
. . . a janitor
. . . a king
. . . a locksmith
. . . a mechanic
. . . a nurse
. . . an operator
. . . a plumber
. . . a quack
. . . a rental agent
. . . a shoemaker
. . . a teacher
. . . a union organizer
. . . a valet
. . . a wrestler
. . . an x-ray technician
. . . a youth worker
. . . a zoo keeper

MORE OCCUPATIONS

I love my love with and A because she's/he's an astronaut.
. . . a belly dancer
. . . a ceramist
. . . a dentist
. . . an electrician
. . . a fishmonger
. . . a glass blower

... a hairdresser
... an ichthyologist
... a judge
... a kindergarten teacher
... a lawyer
... a magician
... a night security guard
... an oboe player
... a pilot
... a queen
... a race car driver
... a saxophonist
... a taxidermist
... an umbrella maker
... a veternarian
... a wig maker
... a xylophone player
... a yo-yo champion
... a zoologist

ADJECTIVES

I love my love with an A because she's/he's
... adorable
... bashful
... competent
... dependable
... energetic
... fast
... gargantuan
... hospitable
... idiotic
... joyous
... kind
... looney
... mischievous
... nifty
... ordinary
... pushy

. . . quiet
. . . rich
. . . silly
. . . tempermental
. . . ugly
. . . valiant
. . . wishy-washy
. . . x-rated
. . . young
. . . zealous

NATIONALITIES

. . . Argentinian
. . . Barbadian
. . . Canadian
. . . Danish
. . . English
. . . French
. . . Greek
. . . Hungarian
. . . Israeli
. . . Japanese
. . . Korean
. . . Latvian
. . . Mohawk
. . . Norwegian
. . . Ojibway
. . . Portuguese
. . . Quebecois
. . . Russian
. . . Swiss
. . . Turkish
. . . Ukrainian
. . . Venezuelan
. . . Welsh
. . . Xosan
. . . Yugoslavian
. . . Zimbabwean

SCRAMBLED WORDS

At the root of many children's spelling problems is the inability to register and remember the precise order of letters in words. Word play — fostered by games of anagrams and scrambled words — sensitizes children to, and heightens their awareness of, the way words are constructed. By solving the problems (and creating their own), children's attention is directed more precisely to the exact letters in a word and their order.

In anagram activities both the constructor and the solver have to pay close attention to correct letter order.

It is more fun if creators of this kind of puzzle try to make the scrambled word phonetically plausible — producing another word or at least a readable non-word. For example, for making a list of TRIFUS (fruits), the words might include CHEAP (but not HAPCE), LUMP (but not MUPL), GERANO (but not ANOEGR).

The unscrambler is helped by knowing something about the word that has to be unscrambled. That's why I like to list them in categories or build them around special occasions. The activity then not only increases spelling skill, but may aid in vocabulary building and classifying.

I am including some of the lists I have made up and used as homework assignments.

MINALAS (animals)

DRIB
SHIF
NOIL
LEAS
RIGET
YONKEM
FRAGIFE
TENAHELP

TRUIFS (fruits)

LUMP
PLAPE
REAP
PAGER
WIKI

GONERA
ONELM
IPENPELAP
RYCHER
WARTSRYBER

STELEGABEV (vegetables)

OTATOP
ROTCAR
APE
RYELEC
CLETUET
SPARPIN
RUTPIN
NABE
CHIZICUN
NONOI

MINALA GOUNY (animal young)

BALM
TITENK
YUPPP
FLAC
TOLC
DIK
CICHK
GLINGOS
LOPEDAT
UNBYN

SCRAMBLED WORDS ANSWERS

ANIMALS
bird
fish
lion
seal
tiger
monkey
giraffe
elephant

VEGETABLES
potato
carrot
pea
celery
lettuce
parsnip
turnip
bean
zucchini
onion

FRUITS
plum
apple
pear
grape
kiwi
orange
melon
pineapple
cherry
strawberry

ANIMAL YOUNG
lamb
kitten
puppy
calf
colt
kid
chick
gosling
tadpole
bunny

ANAGRAMS

Anagrams are always fun. The typical anagram task is to re-
arrange the letters in a word using all of its letters, and only those
letters, to make another word. This is the basis of a number of
classroom activities as well as some commercial games. I especially like the puzzles in which you have to discover a pair of
words that are anagrams. These are usually sentences with two
blanks, e.g., At ten o'clock the story-teller said it was too ——
for another —— (late, tale). These, with the clues only in the
meaning, are too hard for the children I know. To provide more
clues, I have built anagram activities into rhymes, so that the
rhyme itself can act as a clue to one of the anagram pair.

The reason I'm getting a cat:
There's an —— to catching a ——.

Three little bones that help you hear
——— all located in your ———.

Eating cherries won't give you fits
If you're always careful to ———— out the ————.

I urge you to purchase a —————;
The price is not out of your reach.
In fact buy a heap,
They're fantastically ——————.
The price is a mere five cents each.

I've made 10 ———— of soup
They're filled to the top
Now I'm fed-up with cooking —
I'm going to ————.

"I still recall," her husband said,
"The morning that we two were ———."
"The morning that I married you
The grass was drenched with sparkling ———."

I took a ———— of medicine
The strongest that there was —
It cured my splitting headache
Just as it always ————.

——— made all the animals,
Each horse and cow and hog,
The elephant, the lion,
And man's best friend, the ———

Here's the book that I promised to ———— you, my ————.
But remember, as soon as it's ————,
You're expected to put on your nightgown
And quietly go off to bed.

I can't use this ————;
The mice are too smart.
They've opened it up
And stolen a ————

I didn't know right from ——
And sure —— like a fool,
'Cause my shoes were on the wrong feet
When I got home from school.

She didn't laugh or giggle or sing
But she sure did —— when she saw that ——.

If I —— fly,
I'd be so proud;
I'd fly my plane
Right through a ——.

The word you want has just two ——.
These animals have ferocious howls.
Be on your guard all night and day
To keep the big bad —— away.

The doctor said, "For goodness' sakes,
If you want to cure your pains and ——
Then take these pills. Tonight take two.
They'll —— away the nasty flu."

When the day is cool and crisp and airy
I bring the milk home from the ——;
But if it's hot and the sun is fiery
I linger at home and write in my ——.

I'm not afraid of a single ——,
When the moon and the stars are bright;
But sometimes I get a bit nervous
On a dark and stormy ——.

Professor Paul was heard to mutter
About the slipperiness of butter.
Whenever he tried to butter his ——,
He buttered his long white —— instead.

It was the very last hand and time for bed.
"I'll bet my pig," the farmer said.
When the hand was done,
It was I who'd ——.
As for the sow,
I —— her ——.

––– will help me milk the cow?
I'd do it myself, but I don't know –––.

ANAGRAMS ANSWERS

art, rat
are, ear
spit, pits
peach, cheap
pots, stop
wed, dew
dose, does
God, dog
read, dear, read
trap, part
left, felt
grin, ring
could, cloud
vowels, wolves
aches, chase
dairy, diary
thing, night
bread, beard
won, own, now
who, how

MAKE AS MANY WORDS AS YOU CAN USING ONLY THE LETTERS IN THIS WORD

Many of the children I know shun spelling homework but cheerfully tackle this kind of game that engages them in writing words — and thinking about their spelling. As long as there is a pencil and a piece of paper handy, this game can while away many hours. It can be played as a solitaire or can be given as a challenge (with a record to break). In the Learning Centre where I work, it is often presented as contest of the month, entered enthusiastically by children and adolescents who have severe reading and spelling problems; yet they find this a stress-free way of getting practice in reading and writing words.

When this game is used as a group activity, the more able players model the skills for the less able, introducing new words and defining them, demonstrating how to try out letter patterns and work through them systematically.

Words can be chosen to give children practice with particular letter patterns. I am listing some that I have found particularly productive. I also use words that I want children to get to know well; I am including some of these. After dissecting a word over and over, they invariably remember its structure and certainly recognize it when they meet it.

SPAGHETTI

Two-letter words: is as he it

Three-letter words: the tea his its pig gap tap tag pat pit pet peg gas sag has hag hep hip hit hat tip

Four-letter words: this that ship past pest test pate page gash spit gist gasp gate site stag shag sigh tape gape step

Five-letter words: sight tight paste spate eight spite tithe shape phase state tight

Six-letter words: height

Record to Date

CONCENTRATION	71 words
MEATBALLS	49 words
CHRISTMAS	58 words
HALLOWEEN	48 words
SEPTEMBER	25 words
DANGER	22 words
WASHINGTON	95 words
TELEPHONE	38 words
HOSPITAL	65 words
SASKATCHEWAN	62 words
VALENTINE	36 words

GHOST

This is a spelling game for three or more players. First player thinks of a word and announces its first letter, say M. Second player adds a letter, but must have a word in mind. Play continues in this way with each player adding a letter. The object of the game is to avoid ending a word. Thus, the second player would not say, "E" (thereby spelling ME). If a player is unable to avoid ending a word and must say the final letter, it is a point against him or her. The first time a player ends a word he or she is said to be "G", the second time, "H", the third time "O", then "S", and finally "T", and thus is GHOST and out of the game.

Players are permitted to "bluff" — add a letter without actually having a possible word in mind. The next player in turn may doubt that the opponent has a real word in mind and may ask for the word. If found to be bluffing, the opponent gets a letter penalty ("G", "H", etc.). If the opponent can, in fact, produce a word, the challenger gets the negative point.

A sample game in which four players participated will illustrate the play.

Jody: R (thinking "run")
Jill: A (thinking "rabbit")
Dan: S (thinking "rash")
Peter: C (thinking "rascal")
Jody: A (thinking "rascal")
Jill: You got me. L
(Jill loses this round and is now "G".)

Dan: S (starting over)
Pete: T
Jody: O
Jill: O
Dan: G
Pete: A
Jody: I challenge you
Pete: STOOGARY — it's a kind of feather duster.
Jody: Forget it! There's no such word. You're "G".

Jill: Q (starting new word)
Dan: U
Pete: A
Jody: L
Jill: I
Dan: F
Pete: I
Jody: C
Jill: A
Dan: T
Pete: I
Jody: O
Jill: I guess I'm stuck . . . N. That makes me "H".

TELEPHONE NUMBERS

I once had a professor who was very generous with his time, encouraging students to call him at home if we needed help in tracking down references or advice on knotty problems when we were writing our term papers. He was so accommodating that he had figured out a mnemonic for his phone number so that we never had to look it up. "Just dial UGLY MAX," he said. His name was not Max, nor was he ugly, but the phrase was unforgettable and now, many years later, I, who can remember nobody's number, would have no difficulty getting his. Unfortunately, he has moved to another town.

There has been a recent trend in cities all over Canada and the United States for organizations and institutions to come up with catchy phrases for their phone numbers. There is one city where, if you need help with a drinking problem, you can dial ALCOHOL to get the local chapter of AA (Alcoholics Anonymous). USA TEXT will get you a copy of the half-hour text of an evening news commentator. Listed in one city's newspaper was, 734 — REST, the number to call to register for a seminar that helps you learn how to reduce stress.

This trend was the inspiration for a problem-solving game I invented to get students to learn the phone dial (or push buttons) and to think about spelling.

Players invent mnemonics for numbers for imaginary, but plausible, places they might need to call. But they present only the number. The other players have to figure out the key word or words that act as the mnemonic and guess whose number it is. For example, given the number 932-8437, players, consulting the phone dial, would eventually figure out that the numbers are consistent with the word WEATHER, so the number might belong to the meteorology department.

Below are some sample numbers, and, to make the game a little easier, I might tell you that they include the numbers of:
the optometrist
the box office of the local theatre
the library
the day-care centre
the Russian embassy
the literacy centre
the cleaners
a favourite Chinese restaurant
a favourite Italian restaurant
the gym
the dentist
the bank
the appliance repair service
the travel agent
the number for flight arrivals

although not in that order.

222-9748
243-2587
247-7678
673-4948
393-2273
733-3524
842-5387
688-7768
732-3464
344-7655
337-6748
238-2929
237-6242
683-7383
728-4654

TELEPHONE NUMBERS ANSWERS

BABY SIT (the day-care centre)
CHECK-UP (the dentist)
AIRPORT (flight arrivals)
MR. FIX-IT (appliance repair service)
EYE CARE (optometrist)
RED FLAG (Russian embassy)
TICKETS (box office)
OUT SPOT (cleaners)
READING (literacy centre)
EGG ROLL (Chinese restaurant)
DEPOSIT (bank)
GET AWAY (travel agent)
AEROBIC (the gym)
OVERDUE (the library)
RAVIOLI (the Italian restaurant)

ALLITERATION AND OTHER POETIC DEVICES

Alliteration and rhyme are two of the devices used by poets, sloganeers, and publicists to charm, to entertain, to make memorable, and to sell. Our language is full of well-worn phrases that have lasted for generations, just because they are easily recalled and fun to say.

Some popular phrases that use alliteration are:

rough and ready
rags to riches
sweet sixteen
cash and carry
slow and steady
ship to shore
light and lively
bed and breakfast
love 'em and leave 'em
feast or famine
spic and span
star struck
fast and furious
good as gold

Some well-worn rhyming phrases are:

helter skelter
brain drain
chalk talk
willy nilly

razzle dazzle
slick chick
snug as a bug in a rug
surf and turf
seven come eleven
stop and shop
even Stephen
highways and byways

I introduce children to phrases like these and to the devices that characterize them. Then I suggest they watch for similar phrases in the speech they hear around them and make lists like mine, adding new ones as they meet them, inventing them if they care to.

Increasing their own awareness of how people use words and their sensitivity to poetic techniques generally gives them tools and techniques to use language more skilfully.

TONGUE TWISTERS

There are some wonderful compilations of real tongue twisters that I like to use as reading assignments for children who need lots of practice to build up speed and fluency in their reading. Tongue twisters make good texts because they are short and because they sound so nice when read aloud. Moreover, even the reluctant reader can see the point of reading a tongue twister over and over until he or she can read it like a virtuoso. To encourage the competitive spirit, I usually show off my own virtuosity in the tongue-twister department with my fast and furious rendition of Betty Botter — an alliterative rhyme I have practised very thoroughly.

Betty Botter bought some butter.
"But", she said, "the butter's bitter.
If I put it in my batter
It will make my batter bitter,
But a bit of better butter
That will make my batter better."

So she bought some better butter
Better than the bitter butter
And she put it in her batter
And the batter was not bitter,
So 'twas good that Betty Botter
Bought a bit of better butter.

Many children and adolescents have accepted my challenge and have managed to achieve great skill in their reading of the rhyme, often getting a feeling, for the first time, of what it is like to read with fluency. For some of them, the process of repetitive reading enabled them to learn to spell all those words and even begin to recognize when consonants had to be doubled (BeTTy, baTTer, buTTer, etc.). Reading tongue twisters has been especially good for those youngsters whose articulation is imprecise, who have trouble pronouncing unfamiliar polysyllabic words, who have trouble getting their tongues around complicated sequences of sounds. It probably serves the same function as the old-fashioned elocution lessons I took as a child, in which we practised clear and careful pronunciation.

I and my groups of children have had fun creating our own alliterative sentences and phrases. Many of them were tailor-made to suit an occasion and contain the names of actual people. Most of them do not really twist the tongue like "Betty Botter" or "Peter Piper" or even "black bug's blood and blue bug's blood", but they are fun to say or read aloud. They certainly highlight phonic patterns and, if used for reading or for spelling dictation, make an academic activity seem much more like a game.

Here are some of my favourites:

Silly Sally spilled the soup on Sister Susie's Sunday suit.

Spilled spaghetti spoiled supper.

Shirley Schwartz's shorts are sporty.

Danny dazzles dancers daily.

Stars and stripes; stripes and stars,
Strawberry jam in jelly jars.
Steaks and chops; chops and steaks,
Shops chock full of chocolate shakes.

Chestnuts are the best nuts.

Cheshire cheese should please Louise.

Feeling frisky?
Whisky's risky.

Nettie needs needles for knitting knapsacks.

Paul's pop's purple poppies please people.

Fred's friends freeze French fries.

Biscuits packed in plastic baskets last.

It itches where my stitches were.

It's inexcusable that Scott skips school.

Where is Clarence, Clara's parents' parrot?

No one applauds a plodder.

Math's anathema to Matthew.

Haley hates hailstones and snowstorms.

Leona's leotards are loose.
Tammy's tights are tight.
Susan's sweatsuit's sweaty,
Jean's jeans, though, seem just right.

Jennifer's jokes are jolly.

Esther detests dentists.

A dozen dahlias dazzled Daisy.

Olivia loves liver.

Lindsay Springer spurns sprouts.

In June, July, and January, Jamie juggles jelly jars.

Adam smashed an atom.

Miss Marcy mustn't muss her mattress.

Zoe zealously zaps zebras.

Erin erroneously ate herring.

70

Gerry wraps ginger snaps.

Jack's pockets are jammed with junk.

Jody enjoys Jack's jackets.

Pat's pleated pants are plaid.

Let's lend Linda Lenny's lenses.

Joanna chooses juicy cherries.

Shady chaps stash cash.

Fresh fish freshly fried

Dolly's daddy dawdles.

Rash Russians ration radishes.

A soupçon of Sally's salami soufflé suffices.

Once children have been introduced to alliterative sentences and phrases, they should be encouraged to invent their own. Several children can work together to produce longer and longer versions of a basic sentence. Recently in a real-life context, someone said,
"Real runners run in the rain."
Noticing that that had the makings of a good alliterative sentence, several children who were with me each offered words to expand it. They produced,
Real runners reliably run in the rain.
Real runners rarely run in the rain.
Real runners run in the rain riskily.
Real runners run in the rain ritualistically.
Real road runners rigorously and rigidly run in the rain.
Real runners run in the rain responsibly, but reluctantly.
Real runners refuse to run in the rain.
Real runners regret running in the rain.
Real runners in Roumania recently ran in the rain.

In the process of this kind of activity, there is lots of experimentation with sentence structure, lots of thinking about words from the point of view of both sound and meaning, and plenty of opportunity to practise retrieving words from an inner lexical storehouse.

COLLECTIONS

Always on the look-out for ways to develop vocabulary, I encourage children to make word collections. We select a "domain" — for example, words to describe food, actions, kinds of containers, words to indicate quantity of particular substances (a loaf of bread; a cake of soap). Then, together, over a period of time, we collect as many words as we can to fit the category. Sometimes the collections lend themselves to rhyming or alliterative phrases or even poems. Then we make little booklets, writing each of the words or phrases with an illustration — hand-drawn or cut-out — for each of the entries. These, in turn, become texts for other children to read. They are especially good texts for children with reading difficulties, because the theme and the drawings can serve as prompts and context to aid budding decoding skills. The following are some of my best collections.

EDIBLES

Crunchy, munchy, chewy, slurpy
Juicy, bitey, bubbly, burpy
Fishy, squishy, squashy, squeezy
Dippy, flippy, frosty, freezy
Mashy, splashy, floaty, fluffy
Malty, salty, stringy, stuffy
Bunchy, lunchy, crispy, cracky
Trickly, prickly, sticky, stacky
Drippy, sippy, creamy, crumby
Icy, spicy, yuckie, yummy.

ACTIONS

Riding, running
Sitting, sunning
Hiding, hopping
Starting, stopping
Rocking, rolling
Strumming, strolling
Sitting, soaking
Jumping, joking
Pitching, punching
Lugging, lunching
Waiting, weighing
Pulling, paying
Kicking, cooking
Laughing, looking
Filling, flashing
Spilling, splashing
Sweeping, swinging
Breaking, bringing
Baking, beating
Icing, eating

PEOPLE CAN BE . . .

messy, mopey
muddy, soapy
dawdly, dizzy
bossy, busy
speedy, needy
natty, tweedy
jolly, grumpy
flashy, frumpy
waggly, wiggly
ghastly, giggly
wobbly, witty
pushy, pretty
flighty, funny
silly, sunny
noisy, nosy
ruddy, rosy

scrappy, scary
happy, hairy
crabby, weepy
hungry, sleepy

I have used the next collection as a problem-solving task. Each
container and its contents rhyme. Given the container, the player
has to determine the contents or vice versa.

WHAT'S INSIDE?

crates of ———————
sacks of ———————
racks of ———————
bins of ————
piles of ———————
bowls of ——————
pails of ———————
bales of —————
loads of ——————
jars of ——————
trunk of ————
box of ——————
tray of ———
packs of ——————
dish of ————
pans of ————
rooms of ———————
bags of ————
boats of ——————
plates of ——————
tubs of ————
chests of ——————
nests of ——————
tables of ———————
stables of ———————
pockets of ————————
bunches of ————————
mugs of ————
pools of ——————
books of ——————
stacks of —————

plates
snacks
slacks
pins
files
rolls
snails
nails
toads
stars
junk
socks
hay
jacks
fish
cans
brooms
rags
coats
dates
subs
vests
pests
labels
sables
lockets
lunches
bugs
jewels
crooks
tacks

PARTITIVES AND CONTAINERS

The next collection grew out of a game in which we had to produce an alliterative phrase of the form of "jar of jam", using a partitive word or a container word along with an item with which it can be correctly used. (One could say "a slice of salami", but not "a slice of spinach".)

jar of jam
hunk of ham
piece of pie
slice of salami
bunch of bananas
pot of petunias
cup of coffee
mug of milk
chunk of chocolate
swatch of silk
tube of toothpaste
filet of fish
vase of violets
bowl of borscht
wad of wax
gallon of gas
trunkful of treasures
spoonful of spinach
box of berries
barrel of beer
closetful of clothes
garageful of garbage cans
pad of paper
bouquet of begonias
sip of soda
crumb of cracker

Partitives and containers are fascinating words. These are words which designate a portion or collection of something, but the particular partitive or container is often restricted with respect to its objects. It is fun to try to think of a way to characterize the objects that are typically used with a particular word.

loaf of bread
cake of soap
can of worms
bunch of grapes
glass of milk
cup of coffee
bowl of soup
tube of toothpaste
cube of sugar
pinch of salt
bag of wind
tub of lard
basket of goodies
flash of light
slice of bread
piece of cake
dollop of cream
pack of lies
deck of cards
chest of drawers
jigger of rum
pot of tea
carton of milk
brick of ice cream
tray of ice cubes
catch of fish
drop of water
roll of paper
ball of wool
skein of yarn
clap of thunder
jar of peanut butter
stick of dynamite
pocketful of dreams
hatful of rain

grain of salt
head of lettuce
stalk of celery
bag of bones
saucer of milk
kettle of fish
book of tickets
can of peas
bunch of carrots
sack of potatoes
pat of butter
puddle of water
bouquet of flowers
block of ice
puff of smoke
chew of tobacco
brace of ducks
yoke of oxen
pair of mittens
fifth of scotch
vial of perfume
barrel of monkeys
bar of chocolate
spool of thread
pack of cigarettes
bundle of joy
scoop of ice cream
dab of perfume
dash of seasoning
shock of hair
cast of thousands
house of horrors
flask of brandy
batch of cookies
trickle of water
bale of hay
fleet of taxis
case of beer
crate of oranges
flock of birds

nest of vipers
keg of nails
coat of paint
stack of pancakes
page of arithmetic
garden of roses
lump of clay
roast of beef
tribe of Indians
stein of beer
flute of champagne
horn of plenty
growth of whiskers
tub of lard
thatch of hair
wedge of cheese
sliver of wood
pool of blood
clump of weeds
blob of grease
glob of goo
patch of ice
string of race horses
heap of trouble
pile of dirt
basket of laundry
slab of marble
herd of sheep
swarm of bees
sheet of paper
blade of grass

MNEMONICS

GENERAL FACTS

Word play, especially where rhythm and rhyme are used, can be enlisted to help children learn facts, memorize lists, and remember tricky spellings.

Louis Untermeyer, poet and anthologist, talked of the mnemonic function of rhyme: "One word furnishes the key to the next." Rhythm and rhyme have been used for centuries to help children and adults remember important pieces of information that are hard to learn. Facts are hard to learn by rote when we can't put them into any kind of permanent association, thus we say that "there's no rhyme or reason to it." Mnemonics offer one or the other or both. Here are some of the tried and true ones that have been important to me:

For sorting out the months —
Thirty days hath September
April, June, and November.

I never bother with the next three lines. None of the versions I know scan or even rhyme very well. I know, by default, that the other months, except for February, have 31 days. February, with its idiosyncracies, proves unforgettable.

When I learned to cook I relied on these couplets:

One big T
Is teaspoons three.

When cooking rice
Water's twice.

81

When Canadians went metric, these served me well:

Two and a quarter pounds of ham
Weigh about a kilogram.

A metre's over 3 foot 3;
It's longer than a yard, you see.

For coping with Celsius weather reports, I invented —

If you don't know whether you'll roast or freeze,
Double the number; add thirty degrees.

I haven't had to use the following piece of information, but I'm ready, should the topic ever come up.

Every perfect person owns
Just two hundred and six bones.

Grade One teachers have helped children learn about long vowel sounds with the rhyme

When two vowels go walking
The first one does the talking;
And it says its own name.

The most memorable piece of geography I learned in Grade Four — a great aid in drawing the map of Europe — was

Long-legged Italy
Kicked little Sicily
Into the Mediterranean.

In classes in Manual Training — out-of-bounds to the girls when I went to school — the boys learned practical things like how to use a screwdriver. I managed to pick up some of the lore:

Left is loose,
Right is tight.

This has come in very handy for helping some youngsters remember which is "right" and which is "left". I get them to practise tightening and loosening jar lids while repeating the phrase. Pretty soon they have it down pat. And should they forget which is which on some crucial occasion, all they have to do is rotate their wrist slightly, and they know that if it's in the tightening direction it must be toward the right.

Though not great poetry, the following rhyme has helped countless youngsters remember how to report and interpret longitudinal readings on the map.

To the East
You must increase;
To the West
You must grow less.

I have not been able to memorize too many dates of historic significance, but will never forget

In fourteen hundred and ninety-two
Columbus sailed the ocean blue.

Throughout history, weather lore has been encapsuled in verse. Every community has its favourites. I grew up, and planned picnics, with

Evening red and morning gray
Sets the traveller on his way;
But evening gray and morning red
Brings the rain upon his head.

My children learned the same information in more terse verses:

Red skies at night
Sailors' delight;
Red skies in the morning
Sailors take warning.

Some young friends, less concerned with weather prediction and more with the problems of the eighties, taught me their version;

Red skies in the morning
Pollution's a factor;
Red skies at night
Meltdown at the reactor.

From less cynical rural dwellers in different parts of the country, I have learned these:

When sounds are clear,
Rain is near.

Rain before seven,
Lift before eleven.

When a cow tries to scratch her ear
It means a shower is very near;
When she thumps her ribs with tail
Look for lightning, thunder, hail.

Wind from North West
That is the best;
Wind from North East
Bad for man and beast.

The Northwind doth blow,
And we shall have snow.

In the Caribbean, residents keep track of the hurricane season with

June, too soon.
July, stand by.
August, come it must.
September, remember.
October, all over.

Rainbow to windward, foul falls the day
Rainbow to landward, rain runs away.

Speaking of rainbows, I created a poem to help several youngsters memorize the colours of the rainbow.

The sun shines in the puddles,
And everywhere it's wet.
I see red, orange, yellow, green,
Blue, and violet.

I tried to catch a rainbow,
Put it in my net —
Red, orange, yellow, green,
Blue, and violet.

I said the rainbow colours
To everyone I met:
Red, orange, yellow, green,
Blue and violet.

Many children have told me that they remember the rainbow colours in order with a mnemonic sentence, where the first letter of each word in the sentence is the reminder cue of the colour words in order. The sentence which seems to be very well-known, though somewhat esoteric, is

Richard Of York Gives Battle In Vain.

Since I, personally, do best with rhyme, I made a little couplet for it to help me hang on to it.

Call out the colours that follow the rain;
Richard Of York Gives Battle In Vain.

Mnemonic sentences, where the grammatical structure determines the order, are very helpful to those children who have particular problems in remembering ordered lists. A dyslexic teenager, with severe dysnomia — problems remembering "names" for things, words, concepts — taught me her mnemonic for the cardinal directions:

Never Eat
Shredded Wheat.

She said it while designating four points clockwise from the top of a map.

(N)ever

(W)heat   (E)at

(S)hredded

Sentences like that, made up of words that start with key letters — the initial letters of the words that are to be memorized — help learners of all ages to master lists that are hard to learn by heart in their original form. I never could remember the names of all the planets and their relative distance from the earth until I heard this sentence sung to the tune of "Swanee River",

My Very Educated Mother Just Served Us Nine Pizza Pies

Since then I have had no trouble reciting

Mercury Venus Earth Mars Jupiter Saturn Uranus Neptune Pluto.

Everyone who has studied a musical instrument or taken a course in solfeggio has recited some sentences to help learn the structure of the music staff. The order of lines in the treble clef — E G B D F — is remembered with

Every Good Boy Deserves Fudge;

and the spaces — A C E G — with

All Cows Eat Grass.

The order of sharps on the staff — F C G D A E B — is remembered with

Father Charles Goes Down And Ends Battle.

To remember the order of flats — B E A D G C F — the sentence is reversed:

Battle Ends And Down Goes Charles' Father.

Particularly hard for many of us to get straight, are facts or procedures we learn as pairs. Which is which? When Daylight Saving Time rolls around, do we set the clocks an hour ahead or an hour back? We know that those long thin outcroppings in caves are stalactites and stalagmites, but which grow down and which grow up?
For Daylight Saving Time, I rely on

Spring forward;
Fall back.

I get my stalactites and stalagmites sorted out by remembering that the G in stalagmites reminds me of "ground" and the C in stalactites makes me think of "ceiling". Then I reinforce it with this rhyme:

StalaGmites Grow out of the Ground
While stalaCtites on the Ceiling are found.

A school teacher taught me a much more vivid mnemonic for distinguishing between stalactites and stalagmites.

The mites go up and the tights go down.

A chemistry student learning the difference between oxidation and reduction taught me:

LEO the lion says GER.
Loss of Electrons is Oxidation,
Gain of Electrons is Reduction.

I have thought up some sentences that can assist children who have difficulty memorizing the months of the year. Those 12 unrelated words that have to be learned in order pose extreme difficulty for many children and adolescents with learning disabilities. Several young adults whom I counselled, already in university, were still unable to recite the months. For those students who are having difficulty, I suggest that they learn them in two groups — six at a time. As an aid I offer, for the first six months —

Jack Frost Moves Away Most Junes,

and for the last six months —

Just After Swimming Otto Nearly Died.

Sometimes the initial letters of a series of words to be memorized can be made into a single key word that acts as a reminder. Children all over Canada remember the names of the Great Lakes by prompting themselves with the word HOMES. The letters stand for Huron, Ontario, Michigan, Erie, and Superior.

Should a student feel patronized by these teaching aids, I remind them that **medical students use mnemonics like these in every phase of their training.**

To learn the cranial nerves (olfactory, opthalmic, oculomotor, trigeminal, trochlear, abducens, facial, acoustic, glossal-pharyngial, vagus, accessory, hypoglossal), they say,

Oh Oh Oh, To Touch And Feel A Great Violin — Ah Heaven!

And to remember the parts of the brachial plexus (roots, trunks, divisions, cords, branches), all they have to do is repeat

Robert Taylor Drinks Cold Beer.

Later, when they start treating people they use key words to remind them of important clinical procedures. I only know a couple of them. The foods for a bland diet — following a stomach upset, for example, are summed up in the word

BRAT — banana, rice, applesauce, toast.

The treatment for a sprained ankle is contained in the word

RICE — rest, ice, compression, elevation.

Engineers have to remember the colour coding in resistors, where the colours Black, Brown, Red, Orange, Yellow, Green, Blue, Violet, Grey, and White stand for the numbers from zero to nine and indicate a resistor's capacity. Their mnemonic goes like this;

Bad Boys Rob Our Young Girls, But Violet Gives Willingly.

Law students, who have an enormous memory load, rely on a number of shortcuts. The one reminder word I know is OCEAN. The letters stand for the criteria for adverse possession — which I understand to mean something like squatter's rights. Adverse possession (or squatter's rights to a property) hold when the occupation has been

Open, Continuous, Exclusive, Actual, and Notorious.

In high school geology courses there is a mnemonic for the scale of relative hardness of minerals. From softest to hardest, the minerals are

Talc, Gypsum, Calcite, Fluoride, Anarthracite, Orthoclase, Quartz, Topaz, Corundum, and Diamond.

The reminder is

Toronto Girls Can Fool Any Old Quaint Tired Civil Detective.

Introductory zoology courses teach a hierarchy of categories for classifying living creatures: Kingdom, Phylum, Class, Order, Family, Genus, Species. The students remember it with

King Philip Came Over From Germany (to) Spain.

Once students are introduced to the idea of mnemonics and acronyms they can have fun making their own. An assignment to come up with a grammatical sentence to help them remember an arbitrary list not only engages them in the act of memorizing, but is a language-building activity in its own right, calling on vocabulary, grammatical knowledge, and imagination.

SPELLING AIDS

Rhymes, mnemonic sentences, and key phrases are often useful in helping children learn tricky spelling patterns. The best ones are those the children create for themselves. Even if they are far-fetched and ridiculous, they are usually effective because they are memorable. My sister, Sybil Schwartz, an outstanding language therapist and reading teacher, told me the following story about a young student of hers. Jennifer had enormous difficulty learning how to spell, but never made a mistake on the rather complicated spelling of her teacher's name — Schwartz. When asked how she remembered it so well, Jennifer said, "First there's SCH like the beginning of SCHool; then there's WART which reminds me of the wart on my foot; then the last letter's Z like the last letter of the alphabet."

Some of the spelling reminders in this collection have been made up by children, some by my colleagues and me, some have been handed down for generations and their origins are unknown.

I before E,
Except after C,
Or when used as a A
As in neighbour or weigh.

a PIEce of PIE

You hEAR with your EAR.

HERE and tHERE

A LIST of LISTeners

TWenty-TWo

MontREAL is a REAL nice place.

Your friEND to the END.

NOW I kNOW.

The princiPAL is your PAL.

He OFTEN buys a book OF TEN tickets.

EVE can't EVEr eat EVEry apple.

I was WED on WEDnesday.

wHAT has a HAT in it.

She says YES with her eYES.

An ISLAND IS LAND with water all around it.

Do U have an aUnt?

Keep an "I" on your frIend.

Let's go TO GET HER TOGETHER.

I like ICE in my juICE.

GarBAGe BAG

What's missing in ch—ch? U R

BR. . .It's cold in FeBRuary.

R U sending me a Valentine in FebRUary?

whose HOSE are tHOSE?

Our HOST saw a gHOST.

You shouldn't cLIMB out on a LIMB.

I ATE the chocolATE.

His hEIGHT is EIGHT feet.

The teACHEr has a headACHE.

My COUNTry can COUNT on me.

If you bANG the door in ANGER, it could mean dANGER.

If you OWN a chair, sit dOWN.

I gave my SON a lesSON.

If you LOSE you cool, cLOSE the door.

DeAD as A Doornail

Dessert has two s's — that's for second helpings.

It's WONderful that you WON.

ONly ONe

My mONEy adds up to ONE dollar.

There's A RAT in sepARATe.

I   DO.
you DO.
she DOes.

An ANT is smaller than a giANT.

An ANT is smaller than an elephANT.

For Canadian children who have to differentiate between the noun and the verb and remember which has which spelling:

Get on the ICE for hockey practICE.

IS it time to practISe?

The words cOULD, shOULD and wOULD are sometimes known as "Oh yoU Little Devil" words.

MNEMONIC SENTENCES FOR TRICKY WORDS

Come Oscar, yoU Like Doughnuts. (could)

A Rat In The House May Eat The Ice Cream. (arithmetic)

George Eliot's Old Grandmother Rode A Pig Home Yesterday. (geography)

Q. What is the friendliest part of white?
A. The HI in the middle.

Q. What kind of B sits on your hand but doesn't sting you?
A. The B at the end of your thumb.

Q. Why is SePTember named Fitness Month?
A. It has PT (physical training) in it.

Q. How does the letter A help a deaf girl?
A. It makes her heAr.

Q. What is the longest word in the English language?
A. Smiles. Because there's a MILE between the first and last letter.

Q. Why is it good to take the letter S to the doctor's office?
A. It makes needles needlesS.

Q. How do you turn words into weapons?
A. Put S at the beginning. (SWORDS)

Q. Why is the letter U never serious?
A. It's always in the middle of fUn.

I had a little dog
He had ONE bONE,
The bone was hidden
Under a stONE.
A big dog dug there
And when he was dONE
The bone was gONE.
My dog had nONE.

A fellow from Sault Ste. Marie
Said spelling is all Greek to me,
Till they learn to spell "soo"
Without any U,
Or an A, or an L, or a T.

Anon.

I can't tell my "b's" from my "d's";
I'm bewildered by signs such as these:
"Beware of the bog";
I thought it said "dog",
Till I sank in it up to my knees.

M.G.

"Which is 'was'? Which is 'saw'?", I asked Paw.
He said, "Son, there's an unwritten law;
If the last letter's W
Then don't let it trouble you;
It's not 'was' that you see, you see 'saw'."

M.G.

The one-l lama,
He's a priest.
The two-l llama,
He's a beast.
And I will bet
A silk pajama
There isn't any
Three-l lllama.

—Ogden Nash

I know many students who have trouble remembering the steps they have to go through in long division: DIVIDE, MULTIPLY, SUBTRACT, COMPARE, BRING DOWN. An outstanding learning-disabilities expert taught me this mnemonic:

Diane Makes Super Chocolate Brownies.

She told me that one of her young students, when she recited it to him, added, "and Cookies", reminding her of one more step: CHECK.

This limerick has helped me hang on to a mathematical fact.

'Tis a favourite project of mine
A new value of pi to assign;
I would fix it at 3
For it's simpler, you see,
Than 3 point 14159.

The following sentence, however, helps the would-be mathematician remember pi to 14 places;

How I want a drink — chocolate, of course, after the heavy chapter involving quantum mechanics.

The number of letters in each word is the key to the numerals of pi: 3.14159265357979.

Learning and mulling about the little poem that follows focuses attention on, and gives practice in, translating numbers into their Roman numeral equivalents.

Take a hundred and one (CI. .)
And to it affix
A half of a dozen,
Or, if you please, six. (. .VI. .)
Add fifty to this (. .L)
And then you will see
What every good boy
To another should be. (CIVIL)

Many children are unable to remember the order in which to perform the mathematical operations in a complex mathematical expression:

parentheses, powers, multiplication, division, addition, subtraction.

There is a handy reminder:

Please Pardon Me, Dear Aunt Sally.

The best mathematical aids that I know come from Barbara Achenbaum, a geometry teacher in New York, who wrote a book of rhymes for her students to enhance their understanding and memory of geometry facts. With her permission, I am passing on a few:

Area of a Triangle
Triangles, all triangles
Acute, obtuse, or right,
Their area is always
One half the base times height.

Sum of the Angles of a Triangle
I'm giving you a fact, my friend,
It's short, but still it's weighty,
The angles of a triangle
Sum always to 180.

Circumference of a Circle
When you travel round a circle
You won't go very far;
You'll be back where you started
When you've travelled 2 PI r.

Formula for Area of a Circle
The shape of a circle with none can compare,
It's area's always just PI times R square.

Q. If 12 make a dozen, how many make a million?
A. Very few.

Q. Why should the number 288 never be mentioned in company?
A. Because it's two gross.

SECRET LANGUAGES

Collectors of folklore, researchers in child development, and linguists have documented the prevalence of secret languages, invented and used by children and adolescents in many different language communities around the world. This elaborate form of speech play helps consolidate social relationships and gives a group a sense of solidarity. Moreover, it gives its members a specific kind of linguistic awareness. Most of the secret languages of childhood demand some kind of manipulation of the segments of words or syllables — the actual phonemes of which spoken words are composed — or the letters with which they are spelled.

Although secret languages are usually learned from peers (long after the adults in the child's world have forgotten them), there are reasons for parents and teachers to introduce them in a playful context: they provide intergenerational fun; they give children skills to share with friends (some children may need a little adult help to catch on to the secret languages their friends are using); and they offer important insights into the sound system of the standard language — an aid to better reading and spelling.

What to do with a secret language

1. Carry on a conversation with a friend. Challenge others to figure it out.
2. Write a message in the language.
3. Read a message in the language.
4. Write out the months of the year, days of the week, etc.
5. Transcribe a story, poem, or factual lesson. Have a co-speaker translate it.
6. Write out spelling words in the secret language.

PIG LATIN

Ooday ouyay eakspay igpay atinlay?

If the answer to the question is "esyay", you need read no further.

Pig Latin is the most widely spoken secret language. Children usually learn it by listening, discovering that the secret lies in taking the first sound of a word, moving it to the end, and adding "ay" to make a new syllable. For example, "boy" becomes "oybay"; "girl" becomes "irlgay"; and "mother" becomes "othermay". If a word begins with a vowel, there is no change in the word itself, but the syllable "way" is added. "Apple" becomes "appleway".

"Ooday ouyay ontway anway appleway?" translates to "Do you want an apple?"

Note that Pig Latin is based on sound not spelling, and that to convey the spoken sound, I altered the spelling of "ontway" (want).

The most interesting thing about Pig Latin, from the point of view of understanding children's sensitivity to the English sound system, is the way it handles initial consonant clusters or blends — br, bl, sp, st, tr, qu, etc. These are treated as a single unit.

spoon	oonspay
brick	ickbray
flower	owerflay
queen	eenquay
three	eethray

This tendency has implications for the teaching of spelling. Children who have spelling difficulties frequently make spelling errors on the initial clusters. They tend to omit the second member of the pair (e.g., stop — sop; friend — fend). It is as though they were unable to analyze the cluster into its component elements. The Pig Latin treatment suggests that the cluster be taught as a unit of sound that, like *ch*, *sh*, and *th*, happens to be spelled with two letters. Play with Pig Latin, itself, helps make the beginning reader and speller aware of the initial segments in words. Written Pig Latin messages make excellent texts for practising phonic skills. The task is one of pure decoding, where the reader cannot rely on a stored "sight" vocabulary, but must call up an auditory version of each written word in order to restore it to its English equivalent.

Here is one example to decode:

Imay avouritefay omickcay ipstray isway oonesburyday. Utsway oursyay?

Adolescents, given such assignments, who might think Pig Latin is for little kids, will be pleased to know that, in university computer classes, budding programmers are often required to write programs to turn English into Pig Latin.

HUSH

HUSH is an orally spelled language, with the letters coded. The code is fairly transparent, but skilled speakers of HUSH can go so quickly that the uninitiated have a great deal of trouble following them. Though HUSH is normally not writtten, here is a HUSHian text to be read aloud:

Wash hush e nun I wash a sus a lul i tut tut lul e gug i rur lul mum yak fuf rur i e nun dud sus a nun dud I sus pup o kak e tut hush i sus lul a nun gug u a gug e.

It should be apparent that consonant letter names are changed, but normal vowel names are retained. Most consonant names are a syllable beginning and ending with the letter itself, with the vowel "u" in between. Thus,

b	bub
d	dud
f	fuf
g	gug

The exceptions to this rule are

c	cash
h	hush
k	kak
q	quack
w	wash

Nun o wash dud o yak o u sus pup e a kak hush a sus hush?

DOUBLE DUTCH

Double Dutch practises the ability to isolate the initial sounds of words. After the first segment (sound element) of each syllable two syllables are inserted. They are pronounced "ee-uz". So, for instance, "boy' becomes "beeuzoy"; "man" becomes "meeuzan". For words beginning with a vowel, "eeuz" is inserted initially. Here are a couple of lines from a well-known nursery rhyme in Double Dutch. Remember that Double Dutch is an oral language and that the words are spelled here as they ought to be pronounced.

Jeeuzack eeuzand Jeeuzil weeuzent eeuzup theeuzuh heeuzill
Teeuzoo feeuzetch eeuzuh peeuzail eeuzov weeuzoter.
Jeeuzack feeuzell deeuzown eeuzand breeuzoke heeuzis creeuzown
Eeuzand Jeeuzill keeuzame teeuzumbling eeuzafter.

Note that in Double Dutch, as in Pig Latin, initial consonant clusters (bl, br, cl, cr, sp, etc.) are treated as a single segment (broke = breeuzoke).

ADVANCED DOUBLE DUTCH

In this version, the insert is made after the initial segment of each syllable. Polysyllabic words can become very unwieldy, but this adds to the fun. It also gives practice in syllabification. Here is a mathematical fact in Advanced Double Dutch:

Eeuzeeleeuzeveeuzen teeuzimes tweeuzelve eeuzeequeeuzals weeuzun heeuzundreeuzed eeuzand theeuzirteeuzee teeuzoo. (11x12 = 132)

SIPGOH

In this language, only polysyllabic words are coded. It is a good language for gossip, changing only the high information words — names of people, places, and the occasional polysyllabic noun, verb, or adjective. Here are some names of other words and their SIPGOH versions.

Marie	Reemah
Daniel	Yeldan
Louise	Weezlou
Andrea	Adreean
Margaret	Etgarmar
Peter	Terpee
Canada	Danaca
spaghetti	teegetspa
invitation	shuntavi-in

A dialogue in SIPGOH might sound like this:

A. Who is Lee-anat inviting to her teepar?
B. She's asking Tibeh and Enhel. Her thermoh is making her invite Anbry, because he is her zincuh. I hope her therbruh will be there, too.
A. What are you giving her for a zentpreh?
B. A sticklip.

(Translation:
A. Who is Natalie inviting to her party?
B. She's asking Betty and Helen. Her mother is making her ask Brian, because he is her cousin. I hope her brother will be there, too.
A. What are you giving her for a present?
B. A lipstick.)

EGG LATIN

This is another of those languages that inserts a syllable before every vowel sound (not every vowel letter — just the spoken vowel). The key syllable is EGG. The fluent speakers sound weird and wonderful and love to demonstrate their prowess for the uninitiated. Here are the months of the year in Eggeggleggateggin:

Jegganeggueggareggy
Feggebreggueggareggy
Meggarch
Eggapreggil
Meggay
Jeggune
Jegguleggy
Eggaugeggust
Seggepteggembegger
Eggocteggobegger
Neggoveggembegger
Deggeceggembegger

AV

This is a language I learned from German-speaking friends who spoke it as children. The principle is the same in German or English. The syllable AV is inserted before every vowel sound. Here are the days of the week in AV:

Savundavay
Mavondavay
Tavuesdavay
Wavednesdavay
Thavursdavay
Fravidavay
Savatavurdavay

A more complicated and confusing variation on this, for children and adolescents who are skilled spellers and more concerned with the written language, is the insertion of AV before every vowel letter. In this version AV would be inserted before the silent letters in Tuesday and Wednesday.

Tavuavesdavay
Wavednavesdavay

ARP

A friend who grew up in Los Angeles said that this version of the syllable-insertion languages was spoken at her elementary school. In ARP the seasons would sound like this:

warpinter sprarping sarpummer farpall

The cardinal directions are:

narporth sarpouth arpeast warpest

SASKATCHEWAN

Another spelling language, Saskatchewan, uses geographical place names to stand for letters. The name "Saskatchewan" is used after each word to demarcate the separate words. Speakers choose the code word for each letter as they go along. The alphabet letter required determines the initial letter of the city or country. This is one of the ways you could say, "Saskatchewan" in Saskatchewan:

Saratoga Alberta Sarnia Kentucky Africa Tennessee Canada Halifax Edmonton Washington Afghanistan Nevada Saskatchewan

Saskatchewan is generally used as part of a game in which two confederates who speak the language, challenge others to figure out their code. One of the confederates (the receiver) leaves the room. The others think of a famous person. Then the receiver returns and the partner who remained in the room delivers a message in Saskatchewan. The receiver names the person. The other players, listening carefully, and knowing the message to be conveyed feel sure that they can crack the code, but are rarely able to do so. That is because the sender never uses the name of the mystery person, but conveys the identity by some kind of oblique clue. For example, if the character agreed on was Mickey Mouse, the sender might say,

"Finland Argentina Maine England Denmark Saskatchewan Riviera Omaha Detroit Edmonton Newark Taiwan Saskatchewan" — (Famed rodent).

Test your skill and try to identify the famous person that this message indicates.

"Rochester England Louisiana Athabaska Toronto Iowa Vermont Idaho Texas Yarmouth Saskatchewan"
(Answer: Albert Einstein)

OIL ROMJWOG

OIL ROMJWOG was invented in Montreal by a 12-year-old boy named Arthur Rotman. He taught it to a few friends and allowed others to discover the principles. It became the secret language of a group of adolescents in Montreal in the late forties and early fifties. I was one of the fluent speakers. We all put it away in adult life and then reactivated it to tantalize our own children. It was not until I did graduate work in linguistics that I realized how brilliant the language was and how much insight that 12-year-old-boy had into English phonology when he created Oil Romjwog.

New speakers of Oil Romjwog were seldom taught the language. They learned by listening and had to discover the rules which mapped it onto English. I am going to violate that principle and reveal the code here. Needless to say, I have the permission of the inventor of the language to do so. He is now the executive director of a social agency in New York City. I had not seen or spoken to him in nearly 30 years, but when I phoned to ask if he would give me permission to describe Oil Romjwog in print, he said, "Ab kalt."

For those readers who want to learn the language by figuring it out for themselves, I offer a translation of

The quick brown fox jumped over the lazy dog.
Zoi kwike vloim pakt goimft able zoi roethuh haj.

To aid readers' efforts at decoding, I will point out that it is not the spelling but the sounds that are transformed. The Oil Romjwog translation is spelled as the spoken version should sound. Here are a few other translated phrases:

Hello   Deeray
What's new?   Woist moi?

It's been nice talking to you.
Iste vem mit sakkimje soi yoi.

Each of the English sounds has an Oil Romjwog equivalent. The stop consonant sounds of English and their Romjwog equivalents are:

p	f (pin = fime)
b	v (boy = voo)
t	s (top = saf)
d	h (dog = haj)
d (in word final position)	ch (as in loch) (bad = voch)
k	k (kiss = kite)
g (hard g)	j (give = jibe)

The fricatives and affricates and their equivalents are:

f	p (fact = pox)
v	b (van = bom)
sh	ch (shop = chaff)
th (unvoiced)	z (thick = zike)
th (voiced)	z (this = zite)
s	t (sip = tife)
z	th (zoo = thoi)
ch	sh (chin = shime)

The liquid-consonant equivalents are:

l	r (laugh = roff)
r	l (rug = loij)

Semivowels

w	w (with = wize)
y	y (you = yoi)

Vowel Sounds

ee (as in see)	E (as in ten) (eat = es)
I (as in if)	ai (as in my) (is = ithe)
ay (as in day)	oh (as in boat) (ape = ofe)
a (as in am)	aw (as in awful)(apple = offer)
oo (as in moon)	oi (as in boy) (oops = oift)
ow (as in ouch)	oi (ouch = oish)
U (as in up)	oi (up = oif)
oy (as in boy)	oo (boy = voo)
er (as in purse)	oil (as in oil) (fur = poil)

Ipe yoi kom oimhoiltsomch zite tseemtomt yoi moi may Oil Romjwog.

TRANSLATION: If you can understand this sentence you now know Oil Romjwog.

GRAMMATICAL GAMES

QUESTIONS

This game was taught to me by a Californian who said that he and his friends played it as teenagers. **It is a good game to force participants to think about sentence structure, and about how speech conveys more than literal meaning.**

The object of the game is to carry on a dialogue using only questions. The first person to break the rule is the loser. Or it might be introduced as a game where participants co-operate to produce a dialogue using only questions.

Here is a sample dialogue recorded on the night I learned the game.

Player A. Have you read any good books lately?
Player B. Are you asking me?
A. Do you see anyone else here?
B. Why do you want to know?
A. Am I invading your privacy?
B. Where did you get that idea?
A. Would you mind answering the question, then?
B. Why should I mind?
A. Well, then, have you read any good books lately?
B. What do you mean by good?
A. What do you think I mean?
B. Do you mean morally uplifting?
A. Is that what you think good books are?
B. Isn't that what most people mean?

A. Since when were you so influenced by other people?
B. Since when were you interested in literary criticism?
A. Where did you get the idea that I was interested in literary criticism?
B. Isn't that why you were asking about books?
A. Couldn't I just be starting a friendly conversation?
B. Do you want to be friends?
A. Don't you?
B. Why not?

Here are two more that I made up to demonstrate the possibilities.

1. A. Who was that lady I saw you with last night?
   B. Are you kidding?
   A. What do you mean?
   B. Well, didn't you recognize her?
   A. Should I have?
   B. Well, you know my girlfriend, don't you?
   A. How would I know her?
   B. Weren't you at the dance last year?
   A. Do you mean the party or the dance?
   B. What's the difference?
   A. Weren't you stag at the party?
   B. Do you have me mixed up with someone else?
   A. Who could I possibly mix you up with?
   B. Didn't you once say I looked like John?
   A. Isn't he your cousin?
   B. Where did you get that idea?
   A. Wasn't it you who told me?
   B. Since when do I go around talking about my relatives?
   A. What's wrong with them?
   B. Who said there was anything wrong with them?
   A. Then why are you afraid to talk about them?
   B. Who started this conversation anyway?

2. A. May I have a cookie?
   B. What do you say?
   A. May I have a cookie, please?
   B. May I have a cookie, please, who?
   A. May I have a cookie, please, Mother?
   B. How many have you had already?
   A. What difference does that make?
   B. Isn't it too close to supper?
   A. How soon is supper?
   B. What time is it now?
   A. Where is my watch?
   B. How should I know where your watch is?
   A. Didn't you put it away?
   B. Do you think that that's my job?
   A. Don't you always put away my things?
   B. Don't you think the time has come for you to look after
      your own things?
   A. If I do, can I have a cookie?
   B. Didn't you just have four?
   A. Who told you?
   B. Do you think I was born yesterday?
   A. Well, can I have just one?
   B. Will you be able to eat your supper?
   A. Who cares?

WHAT'S THE QUESTION?

This is not a real game, but it is an activity I have used to elicit language from children who have come to see me for an assessment of their abilities.

I say something like,

"I'm going to give you some answers to questions. For each answer, you have to make up a possible question."

Then I give some examples to make sure the players understand.

Children find it intriguing and enjoy the problem-solving element in the task. When they're good at it, they keep asking for more "answers" so they can try their skill. Even when they have difficulty and can't quite match their questions to the "answers", they seem intrigued by the task. Thus they learn about the constraints implicit in dialogue that determine when an "answer" is suitable to the "question" that precedes it.

Here are some of the "answers" I use to make sure that the children can produce yes — no questions, who, what, when, where, why, which, and how questions, as well as whose, how-come, how-many, and how-often questions, etc. The answers have been chosen to get them to take notice of definite and indefinite articles, pronouns, prepositions, tense, stress, and order of elements in a sentence.

1. blue
2. at home
3. a book
4. in an hour
5. on the table
6. to the store
7. five dollars
8. yesterday
9. the bicycle
10. because they wanted to
11. for a week
12. the green one
13. one of the little girls
14. I did
15. because he wanted it
16. to play with

17. Yes, I want some.
18. They were in an accident.
19. A boy told them.
20. No, I didn't.
21. He's playing baseball.
22. It was stolen.
23. So she could play the piano
24. She saw him at the movies.
25. John gave Sue the car.
26. She plays the piano.
27. I sold the book to Bill.
28. Santa gave the **doll** to Mary.
29. The carpenter's building a tree house.
30. I **did** go there.
31. No, I don't have any.
32. It's the **sink** that the plumber's fixing.
33. He did it for Mary.
34. For himself
35. He's just finished.
36. He's been here for an hour.
37. Something to eat
38. I saw my mother at the movies.
39. Superman can.
40. Tom fell in the well.
41. If you will.
42. John gave the picture to Mary.
43. Santa brought Johnny skates.
44. George is doing it.
45. They **did.**
46. Mine
47. If you want him to.
48. Five kilograms
49. Three weeks ago
50. Not yet.

PRECISION READING

With pencil and paper, some magazine cut-outs, or playing cards, or very simple drawings, some game-like activities can be created that get children to focus on meanings of important words, and to notice details of position, size, space, number, etc. I have produced hundreds of home-made "activity sheets" for students who are reluctant readers, yet need the opportunity to practise their slowly developing skills on a daily basis. A number of years ago, as a co-author of a kit called *Junior Thinklab* by SRA, I had the chance to see some of these kinds of activities presented in particularly charming form by artist Jane Churchill. Some of these are reproduced here to inspire teachers and parents to produce their own.

snake under basket ☐	basket behind snake ☐
snake behind basket ☐	snake in basket ☐
snake on basket ☐	snake around basket ☐
snake beside basket ☐	snake next to basket ☐
basket around snake ☐	basket beside snake ☐

if true.
✗ if not true.

♡ above ☆	heart above star	☐
○ above ♡	heart below circle	☐
☆ ○	star in circle	☐
♡ ○	circle beside heart	☐
○ ♡	heart beside circle	☐
○ above ☆	star below circle	☐
♡ ○	circle above heart	☐
☆ in ○	star in circle	☐
♡ in ☆	star in heart	☐
☆ above ♡	heart below star	☐

Here are the Marvellous McGillys.

✔ if true.
✗ if not true.

□ Milly is beside Billy.

□ Jilly is above Tilly.

□ Willy is below Tilly.

□ Milly is to the right of Tilly.

□ Billy is to the left of Willy.

□ Milly is below Jilly.

□ Billy is above Tilly.

□ Billy is to the right of Willy.

□ Willy is between Fido and Billy.

PERCEPTION AND SPATIAL RELATIONS

In each row, ✗ the word that does not belong.

one	two	to	too
to	three	four	five
eat	ate	tea	cup
six	seven	ate	nine
one	tree	five	seven
life	wife	fork	knife
two	three	for	five

CLASSIFYING

Add the word that belongs to each list.

north south east

knife fork

eyes ears nose

yesterday today

past present

cold warm

breakfast lunch

autumn winter spring

morning afternoon

CLASSIFYING

HAPPILY EVER AFTER

This is a story-telling game in which each player, in turn, adds a line to a story. What makes it funny (sometimes), is that each player adds a line without knowing the previous lines.

The game is played with pencil and paper. The components of the story follow a formula. Each player writes in the first component, folds the paper back so that the writing is not visible, hands it to the player to his or her left, then writes the second part, and so on.

The parts are as follows:
1. Adjective or a series of adjectives or an adjectival phrase describing a man
2. Man's name
   All players then write on the paper.
      MET
3. Adjective or a series of adjectives or an adjectival phrase describing a woman
4. Woman's name
5. (AT, IN, ON) a location.
   All players then write
      HE SAID
6. What he said
      SHE REPLIED
7. What she replied
      THE CONSEQUENCES WERE
8. What happened in the end.
      THE WORLD SAID
9. What the world said.

Players end up with as many stories as there are players. After the last part has been written, each player reads aloud the story he or she has finished.

In the course of playing the game, players learn about "adjectives", a little about writing dialogue, quotation marks (we always include them), as well as the rudiments of story grammar—who, where, what happened, etc.

Here are some of the stories I have accumulated in innumerable games with children, adolescents, and adults.

Tall, blonde, and blue-eyed
Big Bird
MET
Saucy
Mother Goose
Somewhere over the rainbow.
HE SAID,
"What's a nice girl like you doing in a place like this?
SHE REPLIED,
"Do you come here often?"
THE CONSEQUENCES WERE (that)
Everybody went home early.
THE WORLD SAID,
"Oh grow up!"

Fierce and ferocious
Garfield
MET
Witty, but ridiculous
Minnie Mouse
AT
The Teddy Bear's Picnic.
HE SAID,
"Have you ever gone skydiving?"
SHE REPLIED,
"Have a nice day."
THE CONSEQUENCES WERE (that)
They lived happily ever after.
THE WORLD SAID,
"Honesty is the best policy."

Quiet and considerate
Mr. T.
MET
Dreamy, dainty, and delicate
Spider Woman
ON
The sunny side of the street.
HE SAID,
"Where do we go from here?"
SHE REPLIED,
"Don't ask me personal questions."
THE CONSEQUENCES WERE (that)
They both lived to a ripe old age.
THE WORLD SAID,
"It's too bad."

DISCOVERING STRENGTHS

Most children have no sense of how smart they are. **In fact, society sets things up so that children are continually confronted with what they don't know.** We send them to school to be taught to read, to do long division, or to learn the provinces of Canada and their capitals. Dozens of times a day, we let them know that they are too little or too young for something that they want to do. Yet children have many intellectual resources that are unrecognized and unacknowledged by adults in their world. In fact, children themselves are not aware of their own prodigious store of information nor of their capacity to use it to solve a vast array of problems and puzzles.

For more than 30 years, as a clinical child psychologist, I have been asking children questions. Most of the questions are probes for information — part of the stock in trade of the IQ tester: "Who discovered America?" "Where is Chile?" "What does 'belfry' mean?" "At eight cents each, what would three candy bars cost?" Knowing the answers to most of the psychologist's questions depends on having learned and remembered a large number of specific facts. I am struck by **how often we undermine children's confidence by asking them questions they are not yet able to answer** — either because they have not yet learned a specific bit of information or because they have forgotten it. The tests, of course, have been designed with the expectations that most children of a given age will have been exposed to particular kinds of information at home and in school. But all children develop

121

differently. Though of normal intelligence, an individual child may acquire motor or language or problem-solving skills later than his or her age mates. Some very able children have little facility in picking up information from the conversation around them. Some have poor memory for facts that have to be learned by rote. When asked the questions on the standard intelligence test, they begin to feel guilty or embarrassed about the gaps in their knowledge. Even when reassured ("I don't expect you to know all the answers."), they feel that they probably should be able to answer the questions that adults are asking. Even children who have never been taken to see a psychologist are apt to feel relatively incompetent in the face of all the things that they have to learn. Yet children know a good many things that nobody formally assesses, or credits, or even notices. As a result, children themselves are not conscious of their own vast store of information, nor of their capacity for organizing the facts at their disposal.

We can build children's confidence in themselves by helping them discover how much they do know, how able they are to solve problems with information already at their disposal, or easily available in the world around them. Moreover, by asking them to display this knowledge, we let them know that it is valued and that what they know is a tribute to their perceptiveness, memory, recall, sensitivity, and attention to detail.

"Serious Questions" is a collection of questions that children can answer. They call on children's knowledge of their own world — toys, games, television programs, household routines, and the objects and processes in their environment that grab their attention.

Why ask them questions they can answer? For a number of reasons. When children find out that an interrogation does not have to expose their weaknesses, but rather reveals their strengths, they invariably react with more spontaneity and enthusiasm, confidently expanding on their answers and eagerly soliciting more questions.

The questions counteract the passivity of those children who are used to not knowing answers, and who tend to give up whenever an answer is not immediately obvious. With the discovery that they are being asked about things they know, comes a willingness to stretch themselves, to examine their memories, to visualize, to imagine, to look inside themselves, and to figure out things "they didn't know they knew."

The questions are meant to be fun to answer, but they have educational and psychological fringe benefits. I have used them in a variety of ways.

As part of a psychological interview, to supplement a more conventional quizzing, they ensure that there are confidence-building questions, not just questions designed to probe for gaps. I have watched timid, unspontaneous children become expansive and even chatty, as they elaborate on their responses to these questions about subjects close to their hearts, and they offer their personal associations and experiences. These kinds of questions are marvellous icebreakers and can be used by any adult who is establishing a relationship with a child — social workers, counsellors, group leaders, or teachers.

As homework assignments for reluctant readers and writers, they ensure that some reading and writing is done every day. I usually dole them out in writing — 10 at a time — and ask for written answers. This homework is always done. Children willingly work at tasks they can handle. They are pleased to demonstrate their knowledge. I never insist on correct spelling, but I find that, in answering these questions, children, impressed with their own capacities, often consult dictionaries or their parents so that their productions can be still more impressive. And, in this unprecedented attention to writing and spelling, they are invariably getting the kind of practice they need.

I use them to divert and entertain children. They can help to pass the time when families are on a car trip or waiting in the doctor's office or sitting around after dinner. They can be asked orally or given in writing depending on the situation and the ages and abilities of the children.

It is with groups of children that the questions provide most fun. They provoke lively interaction, co-operation, exchange of ideas and experiences. Lots of conversation takes place, the less fluent children learning from the more talkative ones in the group. They are ideal for classroom use, but the questions cut across ages and abilities. I have used them with groups where ages ranged from five to 14. In one case, one of the eight children answering questions had a learning disability and another was mildly retarded. Nevertheless, both children participated fully, had a

123

share in every answer, often offering a unique or highly original suggestion.

With groups, I usually ask the questions in a more open-ended way. Instead of "Name three things that. . .," I am more apt to say, "Name some things that. . ." or "How many things can you think of that. . . ."

"Name some things that fall from the sky," I said to a group of half a dozen youngsters. "Snow", "sleet", "rain", "hail", shouted the teenagers. "Acid rain," said a six year old. "Bird manure," said a ten-year-old boy, reported to have a serious learning disability. He then added, "and dead birds".

"Name some things that go on a bed," I asked the children in a nursery school class of three year olds. The answers came in a rush: "blankets", "sheets", "a pillow", "a bedspread". "Stuffed animals," said the youngest shyly. And one little girl took her thumb out of her mouth long enough to say, "and yourself".

"Name some things that come in groups of 12," I said to a class of nine year olds, expecting "doughnuts" and "eggs", which were immediately forthcoming. But they went on to list months in a year, face cards in a deck, a jury, football players (in Canadian football), the 12 days of Christmas, numbers on the clock, and notes on the scale, justifying or explaining their answers when challenged.

And, because it is like a game, with much shouting and giggling and self-congratulation, everyone's remarks are memorable and all kinds of things are learned in the process.

Because my emphasis has always been on helping children find out what they actually know, I tend to accept their labels, try not to get too technical, and congratulate them on their originality if I get an unexpected response. (When I asked for three foods that begin with the letters "ch" and a dyslexic boy offered "cheese", "Chinese food", and "chewing gum", I didn't quibble).

The questions have been designed to strengthen areas that are basic to academic learning: awareness of language, number, direction, our ways of talking about time, hierarchical groupings, visual perception, and just plain thinking about things. Children who are relatively slow to acquire new words in their active vocabulary, for example, who content themselves with approximations and circumlocutions, need help in learning the precise names for parts of things. They may know "ladder", but not what you call the "steps" on it. However, they may recognize the word when they hear it. So, when asked, "What has a rung?", they may very well come up with the right answer. And the reverse exercise of going from the whole to the part gives them the extra stimulation they need to help make a vaguely known word an active part of their vocabulary.

With similar kinds of questions, children are reminded of the specific words for kinds of activities — not just "cook" but "roast", "broil", "boil", "bake", "fry", "poach", and "barbecue".

It is important for adults to remember that not all children of all ages will be able to answer all of these questions, but it is likely that school-age children will know many of the answers and even pre-schoolers will be able to participate in this kind of quiz. The list of questions here is not exhaustive, and probably some of them — particularly those that deal with television — will become dated and should be replaced by questions that deal with current or local celebrities. Children in rural communities will have their own areas of expertise, about local customs, about planting and harvesting and fishing and hunting. I hope the set of questions here will be a prototype for questions that parents and teachers can create themselves — questions that tap the resources children don't even know they have.

SERIOUS QUESTIONS

1. Name three things you need for going out on a rainy day.
2. Name five parts of the body that are spelled with three letters.
3. Name five different kinds of candy bars.
4. Name six of the colours in the rainbow.
5. Name three things that fall from the sky.
6. Name five punctuation marks.
7. Think of two questions that can be answered by the number 12.
8. Name five things you wear in cold weather and not in hot weather.
9. Think of three words made with all and only the letters in the word STOP.
10. Name four flavours of gum.
11. What are five games played with balls?

12. Name four board games.
13. Name three different ways people can heat houses.
14. Name three foods that start with the letters "ch".
15. Name three kinds of clothes we buy by the pair.
16. Name two kinds of food we buy by the head.
17. Name something we buy by the dozen.
18. Name two animals with spots.
19. Name an animal with stripes.
20. Give the names of two oceans.
21. Think of three insects' names that can be spelled with three letters.
22. Name three makes of Japanese cars.
23. Name four animals with shells.
24. Name three Muppets.
25. Name three jobs where people wear uniforms.
26. Name six foods you can spread on bread.
27. Name three kinds of books where words are in alphabetical order.
28. Name three kinds of clothing that start with the letter "s".
29. Name three kinds of containers that start with the letter "b".
30. Name four different kinds of nuts.
31. Name four things that go on a bed.
32. Name five creatures that lay eggs.
33. Name four parts of a bicycle.
34. Think of six two-letter words.
35. Name two different ways to fly somewhere.
36. Name four different ways to ride somewhere on land.
37. Name four different ways to ride somewhere on water.
38. Name four kinds of fasteners for clothing.
39. Name two card games.
40. Name three kinds of needles.
41. Name three different brands of computers.
42. Name five words that start with the letter "z".
43. Name three kinds of fish that are sold in cans.
44. Name three round things that start with the letter "b".
45. Name three different kinds of bodies of water.
46. Name three games that two people can play.
47. Name three families from television programs.

48. Name two detectives from television.
49. Name three things that begin with the word "fire".
50. Name three different times when people give presents.
51. Name three things that start with the letter "t" that you can see if you look in someone's mouth.
52. Name something that comes in sets of 10.
53. Name two words that start with "cat".
54. Name three things that people sleep on.
55. Name six different things you can switch on and off.
56. What can keys be used for besides opening a door?
57. Name two things in the bathroom that start with the letter "t".
58. Name three kinds of paper that comes in rolls.
59. Name three kinds of pipes, besides the kind that some people smoke.
60. Name three things you always keep in the refrigerator.
61. Name three foods served cold.
62. Name three foods served hot.
63. Name three things that give light.
64. Name two songs which contain the word "farm" or "farmer".
65. Name six flavours of ice cream.
66. Name five parts of the body that come in pairs.
67. Name a few planets.
68. Name three things we buy by the bunch.
69. Name three ways of closing a parcel.
70. Name two things you can see through.
71. Name two household objects on which you turn a handle.
72. Name three things people put in their mouths that are not to be eaten.
73. Name three different kinds of coins.
74. Name a red jewel, a white jewel, and a green jewel.
75. Name three occasions when people send cards.
76. Name three things you can buy in a bakery.
77. Name three things you can buy in a hardware store.
78. Name three things you can buy in a drug store.
79. Name four things you can buy in a grocery store.
80. Name three things you plug into an electrical socket.
81. Name three colours that start with the letter "b".
82. Name a red flower, a yellow flower, and a blue flower.

83. Name something in nature that is blue; something that is green; something that is yellow.
84. Name three things you can eat that don't need a knife, a fork, or a spoon.
85. Name three things you can drink from.
86. Name four things you can put in a salad.
87. What are three different ways you can keep your hands warm on a cold day?
88. What are three ways of getting cool on a hot day?
89. Which month of the year is spelled with the fewest letters?
90. Name three white foods that are usually found on the table at meal time.
91. Name something that comes in a tube.
92. Name something that comes in a jar.
93. Name three uses for paper besides as a writing surface.
94. Name three things you can use to make a fire.
95. Name three things people wear that are like circles.
96. Name three things that can make you sneeze.
97. Name three foods that are good for you.
98. Name three foods that are not good for you.
99. Name three things children learn in school.
100. Name three games children play in the schoolyard.
101. Name three places where you should not go barefoot.
102. Give three reasons why people go to the doctor.
103. Name something that twinkles,
        something that sparkles,
        something that jingles.
104. Name something that drips,
        something that explodes
        something that ticks.
105. Which creature purrs?
        tweets?
        barks?
        neighs?
        hoots?
        snores?
106. Which creature growls?
        howls?
        brays?
        roars?
        crows?

107. Which part of your body do you use when you clap?
                                                   kick?
                                                   wave?
                                                   nod?

108. Which part of your body do you use when you wink?
                                                   shrug?
                                                   sniff?
                                                   pout?
                                                   think?

109. Name three things for which the wind is good.

110. Name two bad things about wind.

111. What tool do you need to slice?
                                 to erase?
                                 to write?
                                 to staple?
                                 to paint?

112. Which tool do you need sweep?
                                 to rake?
                                 to stir?
                                 to water (a lawn)?
                                 to mop?

113. Which tool do you need to sew a seam?
                                 to beat eggs?
                                 to chop down a tree?
                                 to iron a shirt?
                                 to put a nail in the wall?

114. What comes on a spool?

115. What comes in a loaf?

116. What comes in a deck?

117. What do you serve with a scoop?

118. Name something that comes from a mine.

119. Name something you can get from a well.

120. With what do you hit a golf ball?
                                     a tennis ball?
                                     a croquet ball?
                                     a baseball?

121. In which sport do they tackle?
                                 bunt?
                                 dribble?
                                 putt?
                                 serve?

122. What do they call the top person in a school?
     in a police station?
     in a bank?
     in a country?
123. What has a trigger?
124. What has a buckle?
125. What has a combination?
126. What object has hands?
127. What has a pendulum?
128. What has rungs?
129. What has pedals?
130. What has laces?
131. Name a food that can be hardboiled;
     roasted;
     baked;
     broiled;
     boiled;
     poached.
132. Which game do you play with a club?
     a racquet?
     a bat?
     a puck?
133. On which occasion do you say "Trick or treat"?
134. Who is Lucy's brother in the comic strip "Peanuts"?
135. Name a dog from the comics.
136. Who picked a peck of pickled peppers?
137. Where is either Disneyland or Disney World?
138. Why didn't Goldilocks eat the Mama Bear's porridge?
139. In which language do you say "Bonjour"?
140. Who won the race between the hare and the tortoise?
141. Who is Barbie's boyfriend?
142. Which animal jumped over the moon?
143. Think of a nursery rhyme with a cow in it; one with a sheep in it; one with a pig in it.
144. Where can you buy a Big Mac?
145. How many suits in a deck of cards?
146. Which animals' babies are known as puppies?
     kittens?
     calves?
     lambs?
     cubs?

147. Which animals moo?
                    neigh?
                    bark?
                    purr?
148. Which animals start out as tadpoles?
149. Which animals start out as caterpillars?
150. Which animal carries its baby in its pouch?
151. What colours are the keys on a piano?
152. What are the usual colours of the squares on a checkerboard?
153. What do you call the things you use to move a canoe?
154. What lines come next in the song "Row, row, row your boat gently down the stream"?
155. Who is asked the question, in the song, "Are you sleeping?"
156. On which common objects around the house do you find bristles?
     teeth?
     knobs?
     switches?
     hooks?
157. On which animals can you find fins?
                              gills?
                              tentacles?
                              claws?
                              antennae (feelers)?
158. If you see a picture of a cigarette with a circle around it and a line drawn through the cigarette, what does it mean?
159. What do you call one of those places on the highway where you have to put in money in order to drive on that road?
160. How many teeth does a newborn baby have?
161. What cereal goes "snap, crackle, pop"?
162. Who does Miss Piggy love?
163. What brand of gasoline has an "x" in the name?
164. What do these letters have in common: A E I O U?
165. What word can you make using only the letters that stand for the four compass directions?
166. Which is further away — the sun or the moon?
167. What animal hates getting wet?
168. Who said, "Elementary, my dear Watson"?
169. What is another name for Saint Nicholas?

170. What is the next line in the song that begins, "Dashing through the snow. . ."?
171. In which country was pizza invented?
172. What is the favourite food of Bugs Bunny? the Cookie Monster? Popeye?
173. Which substance can make Superman lose his powers?
174. What was the name of Dorothy's dog in *The Wizard of Oz*?
175. Which animal has tusks?
    a pouch?
    a trunk?
    quills?
176. Which animal does a magician usually pull out of a hat?
177. What is the purpose of an escalator?
178. When do you say, "I wish I may, I wish I might, have the wish I wish tonight"?
179. Which two children were lost in the woods because the birds ate their trail of crumbs?
180. Finish this rhyme, "Fee fi fo fum. . ."
181. Where is Buckingham Palace?
182. Which animal has a curly tail?
183. Which animal has a stripe down its back?
184. What is the next line in the rhyme, "The eensy weensy spider went up the water spout. . ."?
185. Which animal has a hump?
186. What is the name of Charlie Brown's dog?
187. What kind of greeting cards with hearts on them do people send each other in February?
188. Which metal sticks to magnets?
189. Which liquid do we put into cars to make them go?
190. Which food is yellow on the outside and white on the inside?
191. Which food is yellow on the inside and white on the outside?
192. Which food is green on the outside and red on the inside?
193. What is used to make a candle?
194. Which holiday goes with each of the following foods:
    turkeys?
    pumpkins?
    candy canes?
    eggs?

195. Name something that has one wheel; something that has two wheels; three wheels; four wheels.
196. Name a living creature with two legs; four legs; six legs; eight legs; a hundred legs.
197. In which colour do parents often dress newborn baby girls?
198. Where did Robin Hood live?
199. Who had so many children she didn't know what to do?
200. What tool is used to sweep floors? to mop floors? to clean teeth?
201. What do you use to cook something when you roast it?
　　　　　　　　　　　　　　　　　　　　when you toast it?
　　　　　　　　　　　　　　　　　　　　when you bake it?
　　　　　　　　　　　　　　　　　　　　when you boil it?
　　　　　　　　　　　　　　　　　　　　when you fry it?
　　　　　　　　　　　　　　　　　　　　when you broil it?
　　　　　　　　　　　　　　　　　when you barbecue it?
202. Who had a magic lamp?
203. Name someone who wears a badge.
204. What does a doctor tell you to say when he or she looks in your mouth?
205. What does a photographer tell you to say when he or she takes your picture?
206. What was the name of the giant gorilla who could climb buildings?
207. Which characters from stories do you recall when you hear of each of these items of clothing: mittens?
　　　　　　　　　　　　　　　　　　　silver skates?
　　　　　　　　　　　　　　　　　　　7-league boots?
　　　　　　　　　　　　　　　　　　　a red cape?
　　　　　　　　　　　　　　　　　　　glass slippers?
　　　　　　　　　　　　　　　　　　　silver buckles?
208. What did a raisin used to be?
209. What did a prune used to be?
210. How many strikes get you out in baseball?
211. Which game is played with five people on a team? with nine? with 11 or 12?
212. Who had three sisters called Flopsy, Mopsy, and Cottontail?
213. What did Miss Muffet sit on?
214. Every fall there are baseball games between the two best teams in the Major Leagues. What are these games called?

215. What sport does Wayne Gretzky play?
216. Which night is hockey night in Canada?
217. Which flower is good for testing, "he (she) loves me, he (she) loves me not"?
218. What do you call a big spoon for serving soup?
219. Which drink is made from beans?
220. Which comes first on an apple tree, blossoms or fruit?
221. What does Campbell's make that comes in a can?
222. What does Kellogg's make that comes in a package?
223. If you enter a marathon, what do you do?
224. At a wedding, what do you call the people getting married?
225. Who said "the sky is falling"?
226. What were the occupations of the three men who went to sea in a tub?
227. What was the name of Wendy's dog in the story of Peter Pan?
228. Which part of your body, in your throat, can get infected and hurt?
229. What is another name for your navel?
230. If you carry bags onto an airplane, how are they examined?
231. Identify these dogs from stories. Who are their owners? Toto; Nana; Snoopy.
232. Name three stories with a wolf in them?
233. In which kind of a store would you buy each of the following: eggs? nails? medicine? shoes? school bag?
234. On which kind of clothing can you find each of the following: a cuff? a collar? a hem? a sleeve?
235. In which season do people make snowmen?
236. In which season do people plant flowers?
237. In which season do people go swimming?
238. In which season do people have to rake leaves?
239. Which number is at the top of the clock face?
240. Which number is at the bottom of the clock face?
241. On which piece of furniture can each of the following be found? — legs, arms, hands, a back.
242. What has a frame?
243. Name something that has a shade.
244. Think of three meanings of the word "rock".
245. Name two kinds of relatives who are not mothers or fathers.

246. Name three kinds of relatives who are female (girls or women).
247. Name three kinds of relatives who are male (boys or men).
248. Which illness gives you swollen cheeks?
249. What is the name of a group of seven stars that you can see in the sky at night and that looks like a pot?
250. What do you call someone who makes his or her voice seem to come out of a dummy?
251. Who lived in a pumpkin? Who lived in a shoe? Who lived in a tower? Who lived in a gingerbread house?
252. On which side of your body is your heart?
253. On which hand do people usually wear their wedding rings?
254. When you sing "Happy Birthday to you", how many times do you sing the words "Happy Birthday"?
255. Which two letters of the alphabet are not on the phone dial?
256. How many black face cards are there in a deck?
257. Which letters of the alphabet are made only of straight lines?
258. On a stoplight which colour is the light at the top?
259. Between 1 and 100, how many numbers have a 4 in them?
260. When a sink has two faucets (taps), on which side is the cold usually found?
261. Which way does the Queen face on Canadian coins?
262. Which animal is pictured on a quarter?
263. How many keys are there on a piano?
264. How many squares are there on a checkerboard?
265. Which numeral, when turned upside town, makes another number?
266. Which numeral, when turned upside down, is the same number?
267. Which letter, when turned upside down, makes another letter?
268. Which letter, when turned upside down, is the same letter?
269. In the calendar, how many months start with the letter "J"?
270. Which size shoes do you wear?
271. If a light is behind you, is your shadow in front of you or behind you?

Index